I0654598

LOVE ON
FIRE

V. Marie

Brock Media, LLC
C. CLEARLY BOOKS

Atlanta, Georgia

Love on Fire

Love on Fire

Published by C. CLEARLY BOOKS a subsidiary of Brock Media, LLC.

ISBN 978-0988944633

Cover image: istockphoto.com
Cover designed by: V. Marie

V. Marie

Love on Fire

Chapters

Love on Fire

prologue

Vanity opened the package easily and it contained a note and a black velvet box. She opened the small box first and a pair of yellow canary diamond earrings glistened before her. Then she read the note:

"Life has purpose."

Her heart skipped a beat and a sigh of relief quietly escaped her lips. She leaned back in the chair, with her eyes closed and remembered the love of her life, Dexter McKnight, whom she still missed every day.

6 months later...

Now moved from LA, the earrings transferred to the drawer of her new San Francisco office. She could not bring herself to look at them, let alone wear them. Besides, it was an assumption that the earrings were from Dexter. The vision of the closed casket funeral never left her mind. Vanity never felt as if things added up. Why? He gave up everything he owned and had worked hard for. There were times when Vanity did not accept his death but did not have the courage to fight. She needed a do-over and she had one. The problem with that was Dexter had a way of appearing in her dreams. Somewhat like the dream, she had last night.

He pulled back the white satin sheets on the bed and enjoyed the view of his beautiful love slave. Vanity saw it in his eyes, that he was thirsty to taste her sweetness. His eyes fixated on her breast, her slim waist and her shaven pussy. He reached out to rub the fuzz on her pussy and slid his middle finger in to test the water. Vanity laid back with her eyes closed. She did not need to see this part. She knew how well he would lick and suck on her clit to make her come. She felt his breath over her. He blew gently to prepare her. His tongue was warm and his lips were full and perfectly fit for her fat cat. He sucked...she moaned....he sucked and licked and she moaned louder. He teased her with his finger and blew cool air from his mouth to calm her. He was not ready for her to come yet. Vanity's breathing slowed down just enough for him to come back to give her the perfect lick and suck combination to take her to her peak. "Ahhhhhhhh...hmmmm..." Vanity let out sensual moans, and he looked up and smiled...she was ready for him to finish the job. She wanted him inside her fully and....

From the sound of her cell phone making its tweet sound, her thoughts jerked back to reality and to the man she met about a year ago at the grand open when she lived in LA. Grant and Vanity relocated to San Francisco at the same time. Vanity was not ready to move in with him, so he rented a condominium not too far but they practically spent every night together for past six month. You would think Vanity was finally starting to move on and fall in love with him but that is not what was happening. Grant was still unable to fulfil the void that Dexter left in her heart over five years ago.

Grant Parker did not hear Vanity talk too much about her life back in Vegas and he did not ask. He did not know about her pregnancy hiccup with the twins or how her love affair with Dexter ended her marriage or how the whole situation almost took her life. Thankfully, he took her word for it when she explained that she was in a major car accident and the kids that came to visit were her godchildren – which was all still true.

Vanity relocated to San Francisco to be closer to her new location and with so much change Vanity kept a lower profile. She traded in her canary yellow Maserati for a leased BMW and she decided to rent a beach house since she did not know how long she would be there. Now divorced, she literally moved where the business took her. Vanity also traded in her view of the Las Vegas Mountains for a daily glimpse of the Pacific Ocean.

Before leaving the office for the day, Vanity's guilty pleasure of thinking about Dexter and the package was quickly put in check. She slipped the earring box deep in her desk and kept the focus on her current life. Grant was a good man and he was single – free and clear. They had fun together, they traveled and the sex was definitely the fulfilment that she needed, especially on the nights Dexter did not visit in her dreams.

"It's time to go." Vanity spoke aloud, grabbing her handbag and heading for the door.

one

ONE MONTH LATER

"Ladies and gentlemen, I present to you St. Christopher's -- San Francisco."

Vanity cut the ribbon that crossed the threshold on the red carpet. Two of the original McKnight partners were remaining and standing by her side as she cut the ribbon. The audience walked into her latest success. The anticipated grand opening of her new restaurant had Vanity and her partners working day and night. After the last opening in Los Angeles, two of the partners sold their portion of the business to go in to other ventures. As much as she liked to have nearly seventy-five percent ownership, that also meant more work for her. The thrill of game day always put Vanity in high stress and adrenaline mode.

"Everything turned out great." Nicole said nudging Vanity's arm as they stood inside the main dining room.

"Thanks for your help, as always." Vanity nudged back.

The two best friends gave each other a girly side hug as they looked around the restaurant at the guests who had arrived for the food, wine tasting and entertainment experience.

The evening was well underway before Grant showed up to support his woman, Vanity. He had to work but he promised to be there as soon as he could. When he walked into the restaurant, he looked around until he found his prize. Vanity wore a white short spaghetti strap dress that fell perfectly on her hips and swayed across her ass as she walked.

"Damn, I love that woman. Tonight has to be the night." He thought. Grant had been contemplating on what night he wanted to propose to her. The ring he bought over a month ago had been burning a hole in his pocket. He was waiting on the perfect moment to propose. His hesitation was his memory of her last marriage and how she had once stated she did not want to remarry. Even though that was nearly a year ago when they met, and things were progressing perfectly, he still had that in the back of his mind.

"Hi, honey." Vanity came up to Grant interrupting his thought and gave him a wet kiss on the lips.

"Hi, babe. Great turn out."

"I would not have it any other way." Vanity said admiring her work.

"I should have known. Is Marcus here?" Grant asked as he looked around the room. Some months ago, Vanity had finally introduced her partners to her boyfriend. Now he felt like one of the guys.

"Yes, he is around here somewhere. Can I get you a drink? I have a table for us over there." Vanity pointed.

"Yes, I can use a stiff one."

"Oh, long day?"

"Long is an understatement. I will tell you about it later."

Vanity escorted Grant to their reserved table before going to the bar to order his drink. She noticed he was a little stiff tonight but she quickly dismissed that thought. Whatever was on his mind, she hoped that he would keep it together and not ruin her night.

Vanity wore her genuine smile as she walked across the room listening at all of the chatter from her guests. The restaurant sat in the heart of Fisherman's Wharf. The neighborhood was known for its great dining but everyone was eager to taste something new. St. Christopher's was that place. Vanity hired a chef from Brazil and her staff came from the best culinary schools in the world. Every detail of this restaurant was to make sure it sat a notch above what the natives and tourist expected in an Italian restaurant. The house band played Latin music and live entertainment with showgirls, like in the movie *Burlesque,* would hit the stage shortly. For the opening show, Vanity flew in one of her favorite's ensembles from Vegas.

Back at the table, Grant greeted Nicole and the other guests he had never met. All of Vanity's restaurant managers from LA, New York, Vegas and DC were there for the opening. They had to see the big reveal of live entertainment at the San Fran location. Over the last five years, Vanity successfully launched four restaurants since the original location in Vegas. Having live entertain was something new and Vanity was excited.

"Hey Nicole, can I talk to you for a minute?" Grant asked.

"Sure."

Grant stood up and waved Nicole to follow him away from the table. He reached inside his blazer jacket and pulled out a velvet box.

"I want to propose to Van tonight."

Nicole put her hand over her mouth, "Oh, my god."

"What?"

"Nothing. I think that's awesome."

"Will she say, yes?"

"Oh, I don't know Grant. I hope you are not going to go by what I think. Follow your heart."

"That's the problem. I think she will stall."

"I can't really lead you on this one Grant." Nicole patted Grant on his bicep and walked away. Grant stood there dumbfounded because he really did not know what to do.

At the bar, Vanity ordered the drink for Grant, a Honey Jack on the rocks. When the bartender brought the drink over, he had two. "Felipe, I ordered one drink."

"I know, Senora, but a gentleman at the other end of the bar sent this one over to you.

"What gentleman?" Vanity looked down at the other end of the bar and did not see anyone.

"He said you like Beefeater with a twist of lime."

Vanity looked down the bar in search of the one man that knew she drank Beefeater. Ever since Dexter, she had not as much as thought about drinking that because that was his favorite, not hers. Was someone playing a sick joke on her?

She took the drink she ordered from the bar and left the Beefeater. She did not plan to drink anything anyway and now that she had a feeling that something was going on, she did not want to take any chances being inebriated.

"Here's your drink, honey." Grant took the cocktail glass from Vanity.

"Thank you. Sit down, sweetie."

"Oh, you know me. I have to mingle. Besides, the show is about to start. You relax and enjoy. I'll be back in a few."

Vanity had intended on looking around a bit more to see if she could put her eyes on anything that remotely pointed to Dexter. As soon as she finished the grand opening, she was going to give a call to Clayton, Dexter's old friend that she never felt comfortable around. If anyone knew anything about what was going on, it was Clayton Taylor.

After the show was over, Vanity and others started to file out of the restaurant. She left the closing up to the restaurant staff so her and Grant could leave early.

Grant had decided that he would not propose at the grand opening but that he would do it – in private. After talking to Nicole, he was even more nervous about it. Her response was less than encouraging but he did not want to delay the inevitable. He wanted to marry Vanity and he needed to know if she wanted to marry him, too.

Grant tailgated Vanity to her rented beach house. The drive down Route 101 was surprising clear and when they arrived at her waterfront home in the Bay area, the sun was on its final descend and would in moments disappear from the earth's view. Pulling up to the driveway, Vanity immediately noticed that there were red rose petals leading from the driveway landing to the smoked glass front door. "Oh, shit." She thought and did not like the looks of this. "What the hell are you up to, Grant?" She thought.   Grant had been acting weird most of the night but she was not sure if this was his doing and that is what made her nervous. Vanity had to play it cool.

From his car, Grant saw the rose petals and he immediately became jealous. He wanted to know whom they were from and what was going on. "What is this?" He said slamming his car door.

"I don't know.   I thought this was your doing." Vanity said looking confused.

"Are you cheating on me?" He jumped to the conclusion.

"No.   Grant, I don't know what this is." Vanity honestly did not know who put the roses there but she sure as hell had an idea.

Instead of going through the garage, Vanity followed the path of roses to the front door. When she reached it, she saw a note:

"You are mine for life."

Grant was reading over her shoulder, "You are mine for life? Who is this from Vanity?"

"Grant we need to talk."

"You damned right we do."

Vanity had avoided telling Grant anything about the love affair she had so many years ago. She failed to tell him that she fell so in love with a married man and that she knew that replacing him with someone else would be difficult under the circumstances. She failed to tell him that somewhere in her being she never felt disconnected from his energy. She owed Grant the truth about the love of her life. She owed Grant the opportunity to move on once he realized that she might never love him the way she loved Dexter. At night when she slept next to Grant, she would dream about Dexter. Their sex still went on in her dreams. She would awake often as if she never let go of the feelings he left within her. She could not wait to fall asleep at night to see if he would be there.

Grant could not get in the door fast enough. He did not even sit down before looking at Vanity for answers. Vanity sat her handbag down on the counter in the kitchen and met Grant back in the living room where he stayed waiting on his answer.

"Sit down, please." She could tell that he was on edge and was not in the mood.

"Just tell me what's going on!" He began to raise his voice.

"Look, don't start raising your voice. I am going to tell you what I think is going on but I will not be badgered by you."

"Fine!" Grant sat down on the arm of the white leather sofa that no one ever sat on – not even him in the whole time he had been dating her.

Vanity started to tell Grant about what happened when she had her accident. She told him about the affair that caused her divorce, the twins that she gave up to her best friend and the ultimate demise of her soul mate Dexter.

"So that is how you got into the restaurant business?"

"Yes, it sort of just fell into my lap."

"Vanity, why didn't you tell me all of this when we met?"

She snickered, "It is a crazy story that even I want to forget sometime."

"Vanity, what does all of that have to do with the rose petals."

"Yea, I told you that I did not know who did it but I plan to find out."

"I don't understand. Dexter is dead. Who else could be doing this?"

"I don't know." She lied. Vanity did not intend to tell Grant everything before she knew what was happening herself. She had to find a way to end this conversation. "Let's go to bed."

Grant was not quite convinced about her not knowing who left the roses but he sure as hell was not going to propose to Vanity now. He had to find out for himself if she was playing him. For now, bed sounded good. He had wanted to put his dick up in her since he seen her in that white dress earlier that evening.

Grant followed Vanity as she pranced through the kitchen to the spiral staircase up to the master level.

The house was two simple levels. A main level, which had a foyer, living room and kitchen. The second level was where Vanity spent most of her time. She had an office, master bedroom, and den.

"This conversation isn't over." Grant said as he smacked Vanity on the ass as they made it to the top of the staircase.

Vanity did not think she could get off so easily, which was fine. She was glad that Grant was on alert. She felt him getting too close and she was not ready for anything permanent.

Love on Fire

Vanity was tired and not in the mood for sex but she knew to keep the peace with Grant she had to give him some pussy. This was "Taking One for the Team" night. If she did not want to raise any more doubt then there was, she would need to get really into it. Any other night, she would say she was tired and that would be it but not tonight.

"Grant I'm going to take a quick shower. You need anything?"

"Yes, your ass to hurry up. I'm horny as hell."

"I'll just be a few minutes."

Vanity took her sweet time in the shower. She was starting to have tangible thoughts about Dexter. For the past years, it was in her dreams but now...something was different. She was suddenly turned off by Grant and turned on by the thought of Dexter and she had not even seen him.

After the shower, she dried off and made it back into the bedroom. Grant propped himself up on the pillow with one arm tucked behind his head. His chest hair was a big turn on for Vanity when they met a year ago. He was a Jamaican native but California raised and he kept a beach body that was out of this world. He had already taken off his boxers and laid naked with the remote in the other hand flipping between Sports Center and CNN.

"Damn, girl. I said hurry up. You took the longest shower ever. You sure you did not break yourself off while you were in there?"

"Oh, stop it. I just have a lot on my mind and I wanted to unwind and please, if I got off in the shower, you would have heard me."

"Then, bring your fine ass over here. I been waiting all day to be with you."

"Aww, Poo...I'm sorry I made you wait." Vanity had already oiled up in the bathroom. She walked across the room so the silhouette from the TV could bounce off her perky breast and tight ass. Her naturally curly locks were still down and a little wet from the shower.

Vanity climbed in bed and leaned over so her ass was positioned right on Grant's side. She ran her fingers through his chest hair. She smelled him; he had on her favorite cologne. She nibbled on his nipples and grabbed for his dick. His moans were awaiting escape from her touch. He lay patiently while Vanity relaxed his mind and body. "Damn, I love when you make love to me." Vanity said nothing as she mounted her man and rode him until he grabbed her hips and came. Tonight, Vanity knew just how to give him what he wanted so he would go to sleep.

"Was that good for you, Poo?"

"Yea, baby. That was good." Within seconds, he was sleeping like a baby.

♥♥♥

There he was again...his nature was surely calling her to him. He stood off in the distance...she could not see his face but she could smell his cologne. He smelled so good. She closed her eyes and inhaled his scent. Then she felt his presence. He slightly rubbed her cheekbone with his two fingers. "You're mine." He whispered in her ear. The warmth of his tongue on her ear made the energy inside her surge. "I'm yours." She said. From behind, his dick made its way into her pussy and she moaned with each stroke. "You're mine." He said again. "Not his." He said affirmatively. "Are you mine?" He questioned. "Yes..." she answered with a moan. He kept a steady rhythm before he reached his orgasm, "You're miiiiine!" He grunted as he slapped her ass from behind.

Vanity sat up in the bed gasping for air.

♥ ♥ ♥

The next morning when Vanity made it to the office, the first thing she did was give a call to Clayton Taylor. Thankfully, she had no reason to make contact with him since that day in the hospital just before the accident, but if anyone knew anything, it would be him. She did not like him then and she was not too keen on contacting him now but she had to find out what was going on.

"Hello?" Vanity said when the man answered.

"I was wondering when you would call me." He answered back.

"Mr. Taylor...."

"Please, call me Clayton." He interrupted.

"Mr. Taylor...Clayton, whoever you are. What is going on? Why are signs of Dexter popping up all of a sudden? Is this some kind of sick joke! Dexter is dead."

"You're right Madame; the Dexter McKnight you know is indeed dead."

"What? What do you mean by that?"

"Exactly what I said, Ms. Rodriguez."

"Sir, I had a specialty drink made for me at the bar last night. I had rose petals laid at my doorstep. What do you mean the Dexter I know is dead? If he is, then who is doing these things?" Vanity was growing agitated by his lack of answers.

"Look, Ms. Rodriguez. I have been sent to give you the messages that you have received. How do you like the diamond studs?"

He does know something. Vanity was starting to think that he was just spewing words without making any sense but he knew something. He knew details. But why?

"They are nice. But again, why are you doing these things?"

"I am not at liberty to discuss any details with you over the phone. You are welcome to meet me for tea at Chateau Van Doh in Downtown LA."

I knew it! He was in California, probably at my grand opening last night. "OK, Clayton but I hope you have answers because I am not in the mood for any games."

"Indeed. Meet me at 6 o'clock this evening."

"I'll be there."

Vanity swiveled around in her office chair to look out the window of her corporate office. She was going to find out what was going on.

Vanity buzzed her assistant, "Leslie, book me a flight to LAX. I need to be there by 4 pm and I'll return in the morning."

Leslie was Vanity's new assistant. After moving to San Francisco, she had to hire a new assistant. The first one did not quite work out; she could not keep up with the demands of the job. After a short search, a referral from one of her business contacts sent Leslie. She was perfect. A graduate from UCLA, who was seeking her masters in culinary arts.

Leslie popped her head in the office doorway, "Ms. Rodriguez, the flight is booked and gets you there around four. Do you need to be picked up from home or will you leave from the office?"

"I'll leave from home. I have to pick up a few things."

"Okay, I've also booked you at the Ritz-Carlton."

"Thanks, Les. I will leave the office in just a few minutes. Cancel my meetings and I'll give you other instructions when I get to LA if I need to."

"Is everything OK?"

"I am not sure yet. Grant doesn't know about this trip so if he does call, let him know it was a last minute meeting about the St. Christopher's LA and leave it at that."

"Yes, ma'am."

"Good." Vanity gave Leslie a firm look that she knew made it clear that no one else was supposed to know anything about her whereabouts.

❤❤❤

"Cole, I have been in contact with one of Dexter's friends."

"What? Why? What is going on?"

"Girl, I am not sure but I need to find out. I'm flying to LA this afternoon to meet him."

"Vanity, wait a minute. What are you going to LA for? Who is this guy? And Dexter is dead so what is this about?"

"Cole, you have all the same questions that I have. I need to go and find out what is going on. Something is not right. I did not tell you about the earrings, rose petals or the drink."

"What...rose petals...earrings and drink?"

"About a year ago when I was still in LA, I received a box and note. It was a pair of five-carat yellow canary diamonds. Only Dexter knew I wanted those. Last night at the opening, I had a drink made that only Dexter would know."

"Van, this is sounding crazy. You know that right. We went to his funeral together."

"Trust me. I know. I am not sure what to think but the one connection I have is Clayton Taylor."

"What about Grant? Is he going with you?"

"No! I don't want him anywhere near this before I find out what's going on myself."

"I'm coming to meet you."

"No you're not. You just got back Vegas so, you stay there with my god babies and I'll keep you posted."

"Vanity, you know I don't like this."

"Yes, I know but I will not do anything without letting you know. You and Leslie are the only two who will know I am going to LA. I will not tell Grant until I get there so he can't attempt to join me either."

"Be safe. Call me if anything comes up."

"I promise."

♥♥♥

At LAX, Leslie had a car service already there to pick her up. Vanity looked for the sign with her name on it but when she approached the sign, the driver looked familiar to her. It was Clayton.

"This better be damned good." Vanity spoke firm and quietly as she followed closely behind Clayton. He did not respond but walked with authority as he led Vanity through the crowded airport. Once they reached the door to ground transportation, a shiny black Bentley awaited them at the curb. The windows were so dark that no one could see inside. Was Dexter in there? Immediately, the hair on her neck began to stand up.

Clayton reached for and opened the rear door of the car. He nodded and that was Vanity's cue to get in. Inside the plush sedan, Vanity was relieved and disappointed at the same time that it was empty. Clayton got in behind her.

"What are you doing?" Vanity asked looking toward the driver's seat.

Clayton knocked on the widow that separated them from the driver and immediately the Bentley pulled away from the curb into traffic exiting the airport.

"Good afternoon to you, Ms. Rodriquez."

"I would ask you how you knew what flight I would be on but I'll just let that slide. You've obviously been watching me."

"That's my job, Ms. Rodriguez."

"What's your job?"

"Making sure you are taken care of."

"Taken care of? Clayton, you have to stop speaking in code and just tell me what the hell is going on."

"Patience, please."

"Patience!" Vanity raised her voice. Something she has not done in years.

Clayton sat back on the leather seat and looked out the window at the traffic as they made their way into downtown LA.

Vanity had grown frustrated but decided to get her emotions in check before she blew any chance of finding out what was going on.

"I have to check into my hotel before dinner."

"We'll stop by the Ritz to get you checked in."

"How do you..." Vanity's question trailed off and she just sat in silence the rest of the way. This was not happening to her, she thought.

❤❤❤

At the Ritz, Vanity sat her overnight bag on the bed. For the last hour, she had been stuck in traffic sharing the same airspace as Clayton and it was a bit eerie. He did not make her comfortable especially, with his knowledge of all her moves. Oh, no. Grant. He had to know about him. Vanity pulled out her phone and called Grant.

"Hi, honey."

"Hi, babe, what's up?"

"I am in LA. We had a random inspection at the restaurant and you know how I am about those."

"Oh." He did not sound convinced.

"I will be back in the morning. I have some other business I need to handle while I'm here also."

"Sure, babe." Grant did not like the sound of Vanity's tone but what could he say.

"When I'm in for the night I'll call you. I'm staying at the Ritz."

"Thanks for the call."

This would be her first night alone in months. Grant was getting attached but that had nothing to do with her being lonely in bed, she was actually getting used to that, too. The thought surprised her.

Downstairs in the lobby, Clayton stood when he saw Vanity approaching. "Are you ready?"

"I am as ready as I'll ever be."

"Good. A change of venue."

"No tea?"

"No, I think dinner would be more appropriate since you've come all this way."

"This better be worth it, Clayton. I am beyond frustrated at this point."

"Well, hopefully a good steak and potatoes will help calm your nerves."

At The Palm, the lively atmosphere was to be expected. The sight of a celebrity sprinkled throughout the dining room was no surprise. Clayton pulled out Vanity's chair as they sat in a quiet corner of the restaurant away from the crowd.

"Ms. Rodriquez, I appreciate your patience and I hope that you will find some solace in what I have to tell you."

"Solace? Clayton, please do better than that. Cut to the chase. I am not a child and I would appreciate you divulging all of the shit you have had me waiting to hear. If I feel like you're bullshitting me, I'm walking out of this damn restaurant."

"Please, calm yourself." Clayton looked around the dining room to see if anyone could hear the outburst. Vanity looked at him with an evil eye because she meant what she said. He had better start talking or she was going to start walking.

"Ms. Rodriquez, I want to first apologize for putting you through this agony but I am doing what I was hired to do..." Clayton started.

V. Marie

After an hour of listening to Clayton tell Vanity what had been transpiring over the past five years, all she could do was sit in silence.

Vanity had to take in all of the information about Dexter's instructions for Clayton. After Vanity left the hospital to catch her flight to Puerto Rico, Dexter gave Clayton explicit instruction to make sure that she made it to her flight safely and to make sure that he kept her in his sight at all times. He left Dexter's bedside and was not there when the bomb went off in his room. He never saw Dexter after that. Clayton had been following Vanity ever since.

"Clayton, but why are these recent things showing up. I don't get that."

"Recently, I received instructions to do those things. I did not know what they meant or where they were coming from."

"What about the rose petals?"

"Yes, those too."

"But why? I mean, I am in a relationship. This is not the best timing to have this type of shit going on." Vanity was using that as a ploy to get more information. She was not too upset about the rose petals as it could slow things down a bit between her and Grant but that was not the point.

"Ms. Rodriquez, I have not made contact with Dexter if that is what you're hoping to hear. I am receiving my instructions in the most peculiar ways and I thought it was time I let you know because I can see this Grant guy, getting very close to you."

"What do you know about Grant?"

"I know that he purchased an engagement ring from Blue Nile about a month ago."

"Oh, no. I knew something was different about him."

"I had not received any instructions since the earrings but the night before the grand opening, I received the instructions to send you the drink and have the roses at your door on your grand opening night."

"Clayton, you do know what this means, don't you?"

"I am suspecting the same but I am not going to speak it because we know that it is illegal in the United States to fake your own death. I mean you have benefited from his insurance policies and people are serving prison time for his murder. You could possibly go to prison."

"Yes, I know. What does this all mean now? How do we find out if he is alive?"

"As good as I am he's better. You knew the family guy and the business man but we have the same street skills and his money was much longer than what you received, trust me."

"Clayton, what do we do now?"

"You will do nothing but continue to live your life. I will worry about tracking these messages. Because now, things are getting a little too close and I don't want your life turned upside down again."

For the first time, Clayton made Vanity feel comfortable. He did not like what was going on either. He reached across the table and touched her still hand. He was genuinely concerned and she felt it.

After dinner, Clayton dropped Vanity off at the Ritz and told her to get back to San Fran. Which she agreed and planned to do first thing in the morning. "I'll be in touch." He said at her door.

Vanity did not say anything when she was behind the door of her room alone but her thoughts were all over the place. The room was too big for her taste now. She had not been in the penthouse of any hotel since her and Dexter spent time together at the

Imagination in Vegas. She vowed that this would be the last time and would tell Leslie not to book a room this size again.

Vanity tried to sleep but she tossed and turned all night. Dexter may be alive. The thought was both exciting and scary. He had been watching her; which that thought made her angry. Then her thoughts went to Grant. He wants to get married. Dexter's timing was premeditated. He was trying to get in the middle of her relationship – her life. That made her even more upset. *"Who does he think he is trying to control my life from where ever he is,"* Vanity thought. With that thought, she sat up in the king size bed and looked out towards the LA skyline that faced her room. Game on.

two

The flight back to San Fran was not as relaxing as Vanity had hoped. She did not rest well and for the first night in months, she did not want to have a dream about Dexter. She had gone from still loving him in his absence to being angry with him. The thought that he may be alive angered her. It was different when it was a fantasy but to think that he has been alive and watching her, frankly it pissed her off. This was not something she planned to be a part of. Grant did not deserve this and she be damned if she allowed Dexter to start dictating her life from afar. He had done that enough but it was time for Vanity to move on and give Grant a chance.

At the airport, she was surprised to see Grant there to greet her in the welcome area. "Hi, honey."

"You did not think I was going to let you arrive without a welcome committee did you?"

"It was just a flight from LA and I've merely been gone for 24 hours."

"I know but I missed you last night." He kissed her deeply and she got the feeling that it was more to it than him just missing her.

"Are you okay, honey?" Vanity asked breaking away from the kiss.

"Yes. I just thought you went away to see about that note and I had to make sure I got a chance to tell you how I feel." He got down on his bended knee and kept Vanity's hand in his. With her free hand, Vanity covered her mouth in shock at what was about to happen.

"Vanity, I know you've been through a lot. I know that I am not him but we have something special and I love you. Will you marry me?"

"Grant..." Vanity, caressed the side of his freshly shaven face, "Yes. I will."

Grant pulled the ring from his jacket pocket and placed the double halo princess cut diamond on her finger and kissed her hand. All of a sudden, the sound of applause erupted around them. He picked up Vanity and spun her around as he kissed her on the lips.

"I love you, too." She said unsure of her feelings.

The rest of the day, Vanity could not stop looking at the beautiful diamond that Grant put on her ring finger. He loved her and he deserved love in return. They had built a relationship and there was nothing stopping Vanity from loving him except Dexter, who was now a phantom. Did she say yes to spite Dexter? Maybe so but right now, Grant was safe and after last night, she realized that she did not want to be alone and if she just gave him a chance, she would not have to be. Getting things sorted out between her and Dexter was a priority and she had to do it soon.

❤❤❤

"He proposed."

"Oh, Van! That's great!" Cole said with excitement.

"You knew didn't you?"

"Well, he asked me if he thought he should. Did you say yes?"

"Yes, I did. I mean, why wouldn't I?"

"You have been so busy lately. I did not think you wanted to get married."

"I was getting comfortable with Grant but he sprung it on me and besides, I got a heads up from Clayton."

"What?"

Vanity regurgitated the evening she had with Clayton and the feelings she had afterwards and that knowing about Grant's plan to propose gave her time to think about it.

"So, what are you going to do? I hope you do not plan to lead Grant on trying to get back at Dexter."

"I have no intentions of that but Cole, I have to see how far this thing with Dexter is going to go and one thing I know for sure. If he is alive he's trying to keep me from getting involved with Grant."

"Vanity, this is dangerous. Don't do this to yourself."

"Do what?"

"Put yourself in more mess with Dexter. The last time you did that you almost died!"

"You don't need to remind me." This conversation was going nowhere. Cole was supposed to say "Congratulations" and leave it at that but that was not happening.

"I'm just saying! Do not fall for this again. I know you loved him but this is a little extreme and Grant is a good man."

"I know sis."

"OK. I am happy for you but that is if you are. If you've accepted the ring to make Dexter jealous, I'm not happy about that."

Vanity ended the conversation without addressing Cole's last statement because she did not know how to. She was happy that she felt like the spell she had been under was starting to unravel; but at the same time that meant she had to start allowing feelings to attach to another man. That was not something that she planned for.

The day did not end with Vanity getting a lot done. She made a few calls about her next venture. She had some foreign investors interested in opening a St. Christopher's in England. The thought of going global with the restaurant was far from her mind but they had been persistent about setting up a meeting. Now with the San Fran location open, she had to start thinking about her next move. Her partners were all for it but it would be her decision because after Dexter's untimely departure, she became the brains behind the operation.

Vanity did not know what to do about her feelings either. Cole did not make matters any better by trying to show her the truth. Even though the truth was always there, it was so easy to deny it. Focusing on business was what she was good at – relationships had not been her strong suit lately.

"Les, please book me a flight for Sunday to London. I'm going to the UK." Vanity spoke through the intercom.

"Yes. I will come in with details as soon as I finalize them." Leslie responded.

❤❤❤

That afternoon when Vanity arrived home, Grant was already at the beach house. He had dinner cooked and Café del Mar music playing in the background. He was in the celebrating mood. In a strange kind of way, Vanity was okay with that. She wanted to get on with her life now more than ever. The waiting she did left her with nothing and now that Dexter could be somewhere out there, the desire to be near him was not the same. She had grown angry with him and that was drawing her closer to Grant, which is how it should have been anyway.

"Hi, honey." Vanity said when she walked into the kitchen from the garage.

"Perfect timing." He responded while removing a dish from the oven.

"What's all this?"

"It's dinner, Van. We have something to celebrate."

"Aww, honey, you shouldn't have."

"Why not?"

"We could have gone out so that someone could have cooked for us."

"I know but I wanted to stay in. I know you have had a busy day and I want to relax. You can tell me about LA over dinner."

Now, that was not something she planned to do. That would ruin the entire mood and she needed to avoid talking about Dexter at all costs. At this point, she did not know if her house was being watched or what he was up to. Bastard! The thoughts alone made her angry again.

"Oh, we can talk about that another day, honey. We have a lot to talk about but LA; we can save that for another day, OK?

"I will hold you to that."

Dinner between Vanity and Grant went over without him noticing her mixed emotional state. They talked about planning a small intimate wedding in about a year. Grant yielded that part of the planning to Vanity. Briefly, they talked about their day and that is when Vanity told Grant about her trip to the UK.

"When are you leaving?"

"Sunday. I have to get some things in order with the partners and we'll probably be out there for at least a week."

"So soon? I wish I could go with you but I have a project to finish up down on the coast and I could not get away on such short notice."

"Oh, that's OK, I don't plan on it being a leisure trip anyway and you would be bored if I end up in meetings all day long."

"Yea, you're right. Well, I have one more surprise for you."

Grant cleared the dishes from the table and grabbed Vanity's hand. He guided her toward the master bedroom. When they reached the top of the stairwell, there were red rose petals leading to the bed. Immediately Vanity's heart skipped a few beats and it must have been obvious because Grant noticed.

"What's wrong?"

"What's all of this?"

Grant could sense anxiety in his fiancé face and he purposely ignored it. He wanted her to anticipate his next move and be on edge. It gave him a sense of control in their relationship. Ever since Grant built up the courage to propose to Vanity, he had all types of thoughts running through his head about who this other man was and how he had her all messed up. Grant had to help her overcome that.

"The things I want to do to you..." he said.

"Grant, please tell me."

On the bed, Vanity spotted a few toys that she had not seen before. Her eyes opened wide when she saw the blindfold, whip and handcuffs.

"Are you down with this?" Grant asked.

"Uh, I guess." Vanity answered very unsure of what Grant was planning to do with her.

"Don't be shy. I have been waiting a long time to show you a different side of me. I see that you need to get your mind off of a few things…for good."

"A few things…" Vanity started but Grant scooped her up and into his arms.

"Don't say another word. Do you understand?"

Vanity nodded.

Grant took full advantage of the moment. He carried her to the bed and sat on the edge still holding her. He was about to make Vanity his…in every way possible.

While in his arms, Vanity could smell his cologne. His scent was hypnotizing. His frame was solid and she felt secure in his embrace. She relaxed in his arms and at that moment, he knew he could do with her what he wanted.

He nudged her cheek with his nose in search of her supple lips. He kissed her softly and did not invade her. He kissed her neck just below her ear. Her head tilted to the side, he nibbled more on her neck leaving a trace of himself for the air to catch. The moment was so pure. The room was satisfyingly quiet. Only the exhales from their mouths filled the room.

Grant laid Vanity on the bed, grabbed the blindfold and placed it over Vanity's eyes.

Grant's eyes widened at the fantasy he was about to fulfill. The women he adored and loved was giving him permission to get kinky and he jumped at the chance. His dick was hard as a rock looking at her sexy frame. He grabbed the vanilla crème from the table and used his finger to rub it on her nipples and down her chest in between her breast. Grant knew exactly where he wanted to taste her body. He ended the happy trail with a dab on the tip of her clit. Vanity wiggled at the tingling she felt when he put the crème over her body. "Be still." Grant commanded.

Vanity obliged. Grant's strong hands rubbed all over her body until he could feel her total relaxation. He was ready to enjoy tasting his woman and hearing her moan from his handy work. In the moment, Vanity was there. She anticipated his every touch and taste of her body.

"Hmmmm..." Grant made the sound as he took a long stroke on her clit. He teased Vanity with his tongue. The blindfold was perfect. Grant was able to lick, massage and lick some more on Vanity's sensitive spots to relax her body completely. Grant pleasured her pussy with his vibrating toy.

"Ooooh…" Vanity made her first sound. The vibrator was soft on her clit but it immediately spiked her energy and Grant teased her more.

"Do you like that baby?"

"Hmmm, yes…baby. I like it." Vanity managed to stay still and enjoy the pleasure. The vibrator was placed perfectly.

"Come to me." Vanity beckoned.

"Not yet…this is my show."

"I want you now…"

"Don't worry. You will be my wife soon…I am going to have this pleasure every night." Grant put the vibrator aside and sucked seductively on her clit. Vanity rubbed the top of his head but laid still enjoying the building of energy in her body.

Grant reached up and pulled back the blindfold. Vanity kept her eyes closed.

"Open your eyes."

Vanity opened them and Grant towered over her. His body shimmered from the night moon in the room. Vanity rubbed his chest and six-pack – her favorite parts of him.

He entered her wet pussy looking into her eyes. Their connection was magnetic. Grant could feel the surge with each stroke against her g-spot. "Yes...baby...I like it like that..." Vanity whispered.

Grant fell into the moment and the tip of his dick tingled until he could feel Vanity's orgasm spill over him. "Yes! Yes! Yes!" Vanity enjoyed the uncontrollable shakes from her orgasm as she grabbed Grant when he exploded inside her.

The room filled with sexual bliss and Grant let out a final sigh as he laid down next to his fiancé.

"Buzzzzz." The intercom startled Vanity from her orgasmic trance.

"Are you expecting someone?" Grant asked.

"No. Are you?" Vanity asked.

"No. Wait here."

Grant grabbed his boxer shorts and left Vanity on the bed to go answer the door while mumbling profanities all the way, "Fuck, who the hell could it be?"

Vanity could not hear any talking but Grant had been down there long enough to have told whomever it was to go away. She got up and pressed the intercom button from the master bedroom console.

"Is everything OK?"

No response.

"Hello...Grant?" She pressed the button again.

Again, nothing.

What the hell? She thought.

Before she could get two feet out of the room, Grant was right in front of her.

"Someone named Clayton is here to see you. Who the hell is he? He said it was urgent and he would not tell me what it was about."

"Grant, please. Let me handle this. I'll be right back."

"The hell you are. I need to know who the fuck this man is coming here demanding to see you."

"Grant! Please. I said I would be back. Let me handle it. It's not what you think."

"Not what I think? You must think I'm an idiot."

"What? No!"

"Go ahead. I'm going to my house tonight, since you're going to be handling business."

"No, don't go."

"I'm out of here."

Grant had already started grabbing his clothes before storming out of the room. Vanity right on his heels but did not say anything more. Grant was right and he did not deserve to be in the dark or in the middle. She let him go.

In the driveway was a black Aston Martin with deathly black tinted windows. Clayton came from the backseat in a suit that looked like he just came from a funeral.

Grant looked at him then kept going toward his truck parked next to the Aston Martin. He looked at Vanity when he pulled out of the driveway in disgust.

Clayton walked up to the door where Vanity stood, "We have a problem, Vanity."

"What is it Clayton?! I mean you cannot pop up at my home like this. I have a life and a fiancé now. This is going to ruin everything I am trying to do." She said throwing her hands in the air.

"I apologize but there has been a development."

"A development!"

"Yes, can we go inside please? I have something to tell you."

Vanity stepped inside and allowed Clayton in behind her. The nice romantic evening that she was having with Grant was over, just like that. It angered Vanity because she knew the primary reason that Clayton would be showing up unannounced was that it had something to do with Dexter.

"Please have a seat." Vanity offered.

"Thank you. I will make this quick."

"Please do. I cannot do this Clayton."

"I understand."

Clayton started to reveal the new development about Dexter. Apparently, someone knew about her international plans coming up because Clayton received an itinerary and tickets to accompany Vanity.

"You mean you have tickets to go to England?"

"Yes, I assume that I am going for a reason because everything unexpected these days are involving you. What kind of business do you have over there?"

"I'm going to look into some potential investors for a new location."

"Oh, I see."

"I see? What? What are you not telling me Clayton?"

"I told you that I was good but Dexter was or should I be saying is better. He's getting you out of the country for a reason Vanity."

"What do you mean? I have been planning this deal for months. I have had video conferences with these investors. Dexter is not involved."

"Vanity, you're not hearing me. Dexter has his hand in this somehow or I would not be going with you – on the same flight."

"Got dammit!"

Vanity was fuming. What was Dexter doing? Vanity was over this ghost of a man already! He angered her. He was now toying with her life and all that she was working to build to move on.

"Sad to say, Vanity but I don't know what moves Dexter is planning. I'm in the dark and I don't like it either so I promise I will try to find an angle before we leave and get back to you."

"Get back to me? We leave in less than 48 hours. This is crazy!"

Vanity sat on the sofa next to Clayton and put her head in her hands. She shook it back and forth and did not say a word.

"It's going to be fine." He said and for the second time he touched Vanity. This time he kept his hand on her shoulder and rubbed it gently...too intimate for Vanity. The feeling was weird to Vanity and she popped her head up and removed his hand from her shoulder.

"I'm sorry...I did not mean..."

"It's okay. Let's just get this trip over with." Vanity stood up and started toward the door to give Clayton the cue that it was time to go. She had to do some thinking where both Grant and Dexter were concerned and tell her partners she would be traveling solo this trip. There is no way they could go now.

"Alright, then. I will see you at the airport."

"OK."

♥♥♥

As Vanity glided through arrivals, Dexter peeked through the door and caught his first glimpse of the women for the past years he had seen through his video surveillance. His love had finally arrived.

As she walked toward the restroom, he took in all of her. Dexter watched her hair sway in the wind as she looked confident with her head held high….it was as if his life had went into slow motion.   Her wide stunning smile that she blessed other airport passengers with made him catch his breath and her deep brown eyes became easier to see the closer she got, mesmerizing him.   Dexter noticed the white dress she wore from the night of her grand opening in the States. He loved the way it looked on her and he had imagined this scenario many times but the vision surpassed even his deepest fantasy.   Dexter's eyes moved slowly down that dress and his senses seemed to be on a level he had not encountered since he left her. He could not believe she was here, in the flesh. Vanity's plunging cleavage, made his mouth immediately dry at the wonder and he felt a stirring unlike any he had felt before. The dress hugged Vanity's natural curves and showed all the assets he had remembered and dreamed about many times over. As Vanity came closer to the restroom door, Dexter's rehearsed words disappeared, stuck, locked deep inside his brain. She looked so elegant, stylish. Sophisticated and he felt unworthy.   He wanted to retreat but it was too late. The last few steps Vanity reached for the door, "Dexter..." she could barely say and threw her arms around him.

The smell of her perfume stirred him and for a second he was dazed, unsure if he was dreaming again. "I've waited years for this moment," he whispered in her ear. "I want you baby and I want you now."   He locked the door behind her.

She pulled back and looked deep into his eyes before moving forward to kiss him, slowly at first. Then harder and deeper, their tongues met and during this brief kiss, they sucked each other's tongues passionately.

She pulled away and led him by the hand, pulling him, looking over her shoulder at him and biting her bottom lip. She led him into a room marked "baby changing".

She lifted her dress and leaned over, against the wall spreading her legs and revealing she was wearing no panties. Dexter took a deep breath, all the waiting and here she was, waiting for him to take her.

He sank to his knees and kissed the back of her stiletto, and then he slowly ran his tongue up the back of Vanity's calf, her knee, along her hamstring. She gently moaned with pleasure. "Oh, baby..." she panted. As Dexter moved slowly towards her pussy he could feel the heat her passion was radiating.

Now at the top of the leg, he paused, Vanity leaned over further, spread her legs wider, giving easier access to her. Dexter could sense Vanity's excitement; her beautiful shaved vagina glistened in that tiny dim room, it looked immaculate and he knew in seconds her flavor would be on his lips. Bending over a little more Vanity awaited Dexter's tongue, he moved slowly towards her and the energy from him ignited her. Dexter remembered her sound, the sweet taste of her pussy on the tip of his tongue.

Vanity remembered Dexter, too. So much that she could not hold her orgasm for long. He sucked on the tip of her clit long, soft, and....

"Ahhhhhh!" Vanity sat up in her bed with electricity running through her body. Her orgasm was real and she had the wet sheets to prove it. The dreams were back.

"What the hell am I going to do?" She said aloud with no one to answer her. The anger that she felt on the outside was obviously in conflict with her subconscious. This was bad, she thought. Very bad.

Her thoughts went to Grant. After Clayton left earlier that evening, she called him but he did not return her call, which left her to fill in the blanks about what he was thinking about the visit. Trying to explain any of this would just make things worse anyway so it was probably best that he did not come back because the truth would not be easy to tell and she could not lie to him.

"Hey, Cole."

"Hey, sis. What's up?"

"I'm going to the UK tomorrow."

"Finally. I was wondering when you would get over there and see about that deal. Those investors have been very interested."

"Yea, well I have been interested too up to now."

"What? What do you mean? What happened?"

Vanity ran down the quick version of what Clayton told her the night before.

"What are you going to do?" Cole asked.

"I am going to go and see what is going on? I have been working for months on this deal and if it's a ploy from Dexter he is going to be in for a rude awakening." Vanity said.

"Vanity, you can't be serious. Something is seriously wrong with this picture. The man seems to be watching your every move. Do you think that this is still love? He is controlling you now. Don't you see it?"

For once, Vanity saw it from a different vantage point. He was in a way, controlling her. Ever since she started getting serious with Grant, he has been popping up. As long as she was keeping Grant at bay, he was fine. Now that things started to get serious, he had been interfering.

"Cole, yes I see that now."

"Then why are you playing into his hand?"

"The deal with the investors could be just a coincidence. I have these people putting money on the table and I can't leave them hanging."

"It is not a real deal."

"You don't know that and neither do I."

"Well, I'm going with you!"

"No. You will stay here and run VanCole and you're my interim contact if anything comes up at St. Christopher's."

"Van, you are insane. You know that?"

"Well, that makes two of us, if you can put up with a friend like me!" They both laughed and finished their conversation about the twins. Talking about the twins that were once growing inside Vanity, being raised by her best friend, was always a delightful conversation. Vanity was able to hear about all the interesting stories Cole had to tell about how they are growing and developing personalities. It sometimes brought tears to her eyes that she was not raising them...the only connection she had to Dexter.

"Well, I take off tomorrow and will be gone for a week. I'll let you know when I land."

"What about Grant? Are you going to call him?"

"No. I'm going to get to the bottom of this."

"Are you at least going to let him know that you've made it to England?"

"I will."

"Good. Safe travels and I will see you when you get back. I will need to see you face to face after this is all over. I'll have my assistant book my ticket for next Monday."

"Sounds good."

After the call, Vanity sat back in the dining chair and looked out the window into the Pacific. The tide was coming in and she loved watching it crash up against the rocks just below her condominium. She went over to the sliding door and opened it to let the sound fill the room. She leaned in the doorway watching and listening as nature did its thing. How beautiful the sound. She closed her eyes and let what was left of the setting sun warm her face. A breeze followed and whipped the strands of hair, which escaped her ponytail, across her face. "Alone again," she thought. The feeling she knew all too well. Her thoughts went back to Dexter and the night she realized he was gone forever. Then her thoughts raced back to the now. Vanity held her hand out looking at the diamond on her finger and thinking...what was she going to do if Dexter was truly alive? She would sure find out because in less than 24 hours when she would be in England to face whatever was coming to her.

three

Vanity and Clayton sat in first class to London, England. Once they started on their descend Vanity's nerves must have gotten the best of her because Clayton noticed her starting to fidget.

"Are you alright Ms. Rodriguez?"

"Yea." Vanity was not honest with Clayton but she did not care. All she thought about was the dream she just had when she arrived in London and met Dexter in the bathroom. She always went to the bathroom after a flight. Most women do. Vanity liked to freshen up her makeup before going out. Today she purposely wore pants and her hair pulled back into a tight ponytail.

"Okay, I see that Leslie booked you at Dunston Hall, that's in Norwich. I checked out the location and it's secluded and from the reviews it's a quite popular." Clayton tried to change the subject but Vanity was not really hearing him. All she could focus on was whether that dream was a premonition or just her subconscious playing another sick joke on her.

"Ladies and gentleman we will be landing in fifteen minutes, please prepare for landing." The British American speaking flight attendant said over the intercom.

Vanity rested her head on the plush head pillow on the back of her first class seat and placed her thoughts on all things positive. This is a restaurant deal. Dexter is dead. Grant is her fiancé. Dexter is dead? The thought came back again. That was not so positive but she knew in order to accept all other things that had to be true. He could not intrude upon her life, not like this. Not when she was finally able to move on without wishing somehow that her life were different – with him. Grant deserved a chance and none of these sudden emotions focused on Dexter were a good sign.

Love on Fire

The plane approached the runway for touch down, Vanity turned her head to look out the window at the gloomy skies. The weather was not looking too good according to the forecast. It looked like it would be cloudy or rain nearly every day. Thankfully, Leslie booked the conference rooms at Dunston Hall so Vanity would not have to travel for her meetings.

"Ding...dong." The sound came from the aircraft letting the passengers know it was safe to remove the safety belts.

Inside the terminal Vanity was a nervous wreck. If anyone were looking for a criminal to exit the plane, she would be a moving target. She looked like she was up to something looking around at all of the other travelers as if they were out to get her. Clayton was right on her heels but he did not look any better. They were both on high alert for anything that remotely pointed to Dexter. With the ladies room in sight, Vanity looked over at it but refused to go inside. She did not want to believe her dream was so real that Dexter would actually be there.

At the baggage conveyor, Clayton received a phone call, "Excuse me." Clayton stepped away from Vanity.

Vanity immediately thought that it was something that had to do with Dexter but when Clayton came back, he did not mention anything.

"Well?" She looked irritated.

"Well, what?"

"Who was that?"

"It was not Dexter. It was my assistant."

"Oh. I didn't know you had an assistant."

"Don't worry Vanity. As soon as I know something I will let you know."

"Yea well at this rate, I am not so sure you will even know any more than I will." Vanity's sarcasm was on full blast.

Clayton did not respond but Vanity was right. It appeared that if Dexter was alive that he had been making moves without involving either of them at this point. As sharp as Clayton was he did not seem bothered by it and that is what worried Vanity.

The airport was in Heathrow an industrial area west of London. They headed toward the M25, which was the London Orbital, a highway that circles the city and then onto M11 headed north. The industrial scenery changed to a pleasant countryside once they hit the A11 toward Norfolk and Anglia. From the long drive, Vanity was able to see the vast farming lands of corn and wheat and the closer they became to Norfolk the smaller the roads became.

When Vanity checked into the hotel, the first thing she did was call Cole to let her and Christina know that she had made it.

"Hey sis."

"You landed?"

"Safe and sound."

"Any sign of him?"

"No. I need to focus on this deal and not focus so much on him. Until I see him, I don't know what the hell is going on."

"Okay. Be careful. Is that Clayton guy there with you?"

"Yes, but he's just as clueless as I am and I cannot understand that."

"He is there to keep his eye on you and that is all that I am concerned about."

"I do feel a little safer with him here. I've traveled a great distance alone and with all of this nonsense going on I am glad to be traveling with someone."

"Have you talked to Grant?"

"No. I haven't since the other night when he left."

"Vanity, what are you going to do? You just accepted his ring. This is starting off badly."

"You don't have to remind me about that. I know and I am going to try to find the underlying cause of this while I am here. If this is a setup, I'll find out in the morning when I am supposed to meet with the investors."

"Keep me posted and you had better give me a call as soon as something happens with the deal or if the ghost from Christmas past shows his face." Cole laughed.

"This is not funny!" Vanity managed a chuckle.

"Oh well, I am trying to make light of this situation since it's all screwed up. Hey, your godchildren are fussing for their snack. What time is it there?"

"Uh, it's just after one o'clock."

"Two hours difference, that's good to know. Please do not call me when I'm sleep unless it's an emergency." Cole laughed again.

"Oh, girl please. I plan to have this meeting tomorrow and see if we can come to an agreement, then get my shop and eat on and get my ass back to the States in a few days."

"Okay. Keep Clayton close by."

"Don't worry I will. Kiss my babies for me."

"Always do. See ya."

"See ya."

Vanity held the phone in her hand a little longer just because she felt so far away from her loved ones. It had been a long time since she traveled abroad alone. It had been even longer since she traveled for business since she did a lot of her prior marketing business in Vegas. Business in England was not something she ever thought that she would be doing but here she was about to look at a restaurant deal with foreign investors.

Before Vanity had a chance to wallow in the moment, there was a knock on the door.

"Who is it?" Vanity asked from the inside of her hotel suite.

"Clayton."

Vanity opened the door without looking through the peephole because no one could sound quite like Clayton. When she opened it, he had on a black suit and dark shades.

"Hi…" Vanity was thrown off guard with the get up and was not sure what it was about. She thought he looked ridiculous.

"Ms. Rodriguez. We have a meeting to attend. Please get dressed."

"What? What kind of meeting? I am not scheduled to meet with my investors until tomorrow morning. I'm a little jet lagged."

"This is not a request."

"Excuse me?"

"There are some things happening that I have just been made aware of. Please just get dressed and meet me outside in ten minutes."

"Ten minutes? Clayton, if you don't tell me what the hell is going on; I will not meet you anywhere!" Vanity was pissed.

"I am not at liberty to provide that information to you."

"Not at liberty or you don't know shit yourself?"

Clayton was clearly irritated by the last statement and instead of commenting he turned and left the room to stand post outside Vanity's door.

"Ten minutes." He said before he closed the door.

"We'll see about that." Vanity spewed under her breath.

Vanity was just about to blow a top. Whom did he think he was telling her to do something without any information? This was not the way things were supposed to be at this point in her life. She was supposed to be in control, not be controlled.

Vanity looked in her luggage for a pair of jeans and a top that said she was not as impressed about this meeting as Clayton was. By the time she emerged from the bathroom with her hair and makeup done, it had been nearly twenty minutes.

She opened the door of her suite and was startled by Clayton standing next to her door like a bodyguard.

"What are you doing by my door?"

"Waiting for you. Let's go."

"At what point did you become my bodyguard."

Clayton did not answer. He kept walking toward the elevator and when they entered it, he did not look back at Vanity, he faced the door and when it opened on the first floor, he stepped aside allowing Vanity to exit in front of him.

"This way." He ordered.

Vanity started to comply with the orders because he was not forthcoming with any information and it was a waste of her breath and patience to continue asking questions. Soon enough she would see whom they would be meeting with.

In the driveway of the hotel was a black Maybach. The windows were so black that the Queen herself could have very well been inside and no one would know it. Clayton pulled the rear passenger door open for Vanity.

Inside, there was a man. A man she did not know nor recognize. The door closed behind her and immediately, Vanity did not like it. She needed Clayton by her side because this was a stranger and she needed to feel safe.

"Do not be alarmed Ms. Rodriguez." The dark skinned Englishman said.

"Who are you and how do you know my name?"

"We have business to take care of."

"Excuse me? You are not one of the executives I am meeting here. Who are you?" Vanity asked again.

"You have two very important things that belongs to my family and I believe you may not know how valuable they are. I have waited patiently to get this meeting with you and I apologize for the cover up."

"Cover up?"

"This trip is not about a new restaurant."

"Oh. Well then you had better get to talking because if I do not know what the fuck is going on in the next five minutes, I am on the next plane back to the San Francisco."

"Calm down, please."

"Calm down? I have traveled to another country under the impression that I am here to make some business moves and you tell me that that was a set up." Vanity was reaching for the door handle when the car started to roll away from the curb.

"Wait! I am not going anywhere with you." The door was locked.

Panic settled in and Vanity did not like the fact that she was driving away from her hotel and she did not see Clayton anywhere in sight. Where did he go?

"Ms. Rodriguez, I am not going to harm you. I need you to calm down so that you do not misunderstand what this is about."

"Why are we leaving the hotel then?"

"We have to talk about it privately.   Clayton will be fine. He knows where we are going. He is following us."

"Clayton is in on this?" Vanity looked out the back window to see another black sedan following closely behind them.

"In on this?" The man chuckled.

"What's so damn funny?"

"Clayton is not in on anything. We're not going too far from Dunston Hall."

Vanity sat looking out the window at the foreign scene. She did not know what "not far" meant. This was not her country and she would not know how to get back to her hotel. In that moment, she realized she had better change her attitude and pay close attention to what was going on around her.

The drive seemed like it was at least fifteen minutes before they arrived at a large mansion. The house sat at least three acres back from the main road. The house was surrounded by a prairie of trees that looked hundreds of years old. It was something Vanity had seen in magazines and on television, nothing like the city lifestyle she was accustomed to. They pulled into the circular driveway and a man stood with a butler's suit on and opened the door for Vanity to exit.

Without a word, Vanity stepped out of the sedan and waited for the mystery man to exit behind her.

"Welcome to my estate."

"Well, I don't even know who you are so I am not all that impressed."

"Very well. This way."

Vanity followed the butler into the house and he escorted her to a sitting room that sat off the main entrance.

"Can I get you something to drink?" A woman in a maid's uniform came out of nowhere.

"No, thank you."

Vanity could not help but to look around at all of the antique furniture. This was definitely a different type of wealth then she had seen in the states. This was what they called, "old money".

"Ms. Rodriguez, Mr. McKnight will see you now." The maid said.

Vanity could not move from her seat. She heard his name and her body lost all of its consciousness and could not move.

"Ma'am? This way, please. We do not want to keep him waiting."

Vanity stood but her legs were like jelly and her hands and face were a tingling mess. She was not ready for this. She followed the maid down the long corridor to an office. When she went into the room, she saw the same man from the car who picked her up at the hotel. She looked passed him and looked for Dexter. He was not in the room.

"Where is Dexter?" Vanity asked the man.

He chuckled.

"Your name? Who are you?"

"I am Drexel McKnight."

"Drexel?"

"Are you related to Dexter? What is this about?"

"Please, Ms. Rodriguez, have a seat. We have a lot to discuss."

"You damned right we do."

"Please refrain from profanities. I want you to respect my position and how I had to handle this to protect all of those involved."

"Well you better get to talking because I have just spent my last bit of patience walking in here."

Drexel stood up, came over to Vanity, and grabbed her hand softly. "Please, come and sit down."

From his touch, she calmed. His energy was genuine and Vanity felt like she could sit and at least listen to him. When they both sat on the high back sofa, Drexel began to tell her why she was in England.

"Vanity, can I call you that?"

"Yes."

"Thank you. I first want to apologize for bringing you so far away from your element but it was for your safety."

"My safety...." She started to question but Drexel put his finger over his lips to silence her.

"Let me finish."

Drexel began to tell Vanity about all of the events that led up to that very moment.

"Francine's cartel family have always tried to get close to my family and our wealth and they have been watching you and my brother's children since you left Vegas and I've had to keep my eye on them and you for him."

Drexel continued, "Dexter and I were separated when we were children, he grew up in the US, and my family never gave up trying to get him back. The Mansell's, Francine's family, found out about our family's lineage and ever since then they had been plotting to get him to put money into their operations. He always refused and practically cut all ties with our family and even stopped visiting us. I found out about your relationship and knew that it would only be a matter of time before they tried to end it because Francine was not the type to let you step in and get what she and her family had been trying to get for years."

"I don't understand what this has to do with me." Vanity interrupted.

"Dexter must have known that something was going to happen with the Mansell family because he contacted me and asked that if something did happen that I make sure that you, Cassidy and Collin were kept safe from it."

"Why am I here, in England? You could have told me this over the phone."

"Vanity, it's more complicated than that. You see, everything that Dexter left you was part of what he was truly worth; but he told me that if something happened to him that I had to keep you and his children safe. He said that he left something with you that would give me assurance that no matter what happened, that he still had your heart and if you had this, I had instructions to take care of you for the rest of your life."

"What? I don't need that! I am moving on with my life."

"Vanity, please. Do you still carry the picture in your wallet?"

"Yes. Why? What does that have to do with anything?"

Vanity went back to the moment in the doctor's office when they found out they were having twins. The doctor gave them both a picture of the budding babies. They both folded the photo and tucked their little "secret" into their wallets.

"My brother said that if you kept that, he knew that he would still have your heart, all these years later."

"Dexter was the love of my life. He knew that. Nothing would change that."

"He said the same thing about you."

"I don't get it. When did he say these things to you?"

"That day in the hospital when you had left to go to the airport to visit your grandmother."

Drexel started to explain that Dexter had an inheritance that was off the books in the United States and the one person that he would give it to was Vanity.

"Drexel, I've already taken enough from Dexter. The restaurant business is a lot of work and enough to manage. I do not think that I need any more from him. I was doing well before I got in the middle of all this. Besides, Dexter has more children than the twins. "

"You do not understand. This is not an offer you can refuse. I am carrying out my brothers wishes. The caveat is that you have to move to England."

"Oh, no!" Vanity yelled.

"Please, do not shout."

"I'm not going into hiding in this country. I like my life in San Francisco. I've just gotten engaged and I am moving on with my life."

"Yea, about that. Grant is not your type."

"What? Who do you think you are? OK, I'm out of here." Vanity stood and started to leave the room and Drexel stood and pleaded with her.

"Please, Vanity. I'm sorry. I should not have said that. I am just looking out for my brother."

"Dexter is dead. He cannot control my life from the grave. This is absurd."

Drexel came over to Vanity and placed a hand on her shoulder, "I understand that this is a lot of information for you take in but I promise you that coming to England is not a bad thing. You will love it here. We can always start the restaurants up here. I've seen your work and you've taken them to another level."

"We? Thank you but this is a lot. You are asking me to leave all that I know to move to a country just to have wealth that does not belong to me. What am I going to tell my fiancé and my family?"

"You can tell them that you have to come here to start the restaurant, which you will and just come and see how you like it."

"Grant is not going to be able to move to England."

"Vanity, this does not extend to Grant or Francine's children. This is for you, the twins, Christina and Nicole and her family, if they want to come."

"So I'm supposed to give up my relationship to have no relationship. This is sounding easier to decline the more you talk about it."

"I have to honor his request. You may find an Englishman to your liking."

"Englishman, huh? If they are as stuffy as you are, then I may as well become a nun."

"Stuffy?"

"Never mind. I would like to go back to my hotel now. I think I have heard enough for one day. So, I guess I'll have the next few days to think about this and do some shopping since I don't have any real business to take care of."

"Clayton will usher you back to the hotel."

"Speaking of Clayton, are you related to him too?

"No. Clayton is a trusted friend of my brother's. I used him because I knew he would get you here safely."

"Yeah, everyone trusts everyone else with information except me."

"I'm sorry for keeping this a secret for so long but it was for your own good that you heard this from me and I could not risk coming there and drawing any attention to you."

"Like a sudden move to England is not attention."

"I have devised a plan should you decide to move that would not do such a thing. Please think about it and give me your answer before you return to the States."

"Oh, you will get an answer. I do not plan to drag this out."

"Thank you. One last thing, do not call your family and discuss this over the phone. You need to make this decision independently and when you return be very careful about who you tell. Remember this is a business venture."

"Right. Business." Vanity thought that this was crazy. She met Clayton by the front door near the foyer. The Maybach pulled up and the butler opened the door for them get inside. Within minutes, the big house was fading into the background as they exited the McKnight estate.

four

For the next few days, Vanity spent time at the McKnight estate learning about the family and all of the interesting things that Dexter never mentioned. He came from a family of carpenters. They owned the oldest construction company in London. Their great great grandfather built the home that Drexel lived in when he started his family.

Dexter's mother was one of the American house servants that got pregnant by Pascal McKnight and when she had the twins she tried to flee back to the States but she was only able to take Dexter. He was still a toddler when she left and never went back but the McKnight's always kept a close eye on Dexter and when he became of age they reached out to him and told him about his real heritage. He rejected them at first until he learned the truth from his mother. By the time he learned about the wealth of his family he had become his own man and did not want anything from them. It took him visiting England to meet his fraternal twin brother Drexel to understand that this was just the way it was. His family was wealthy and because he was a McKnight, he was wealthy, too. From that point, Dexter kept his family a secret from everyone but somehow Francine's family learned about Dexter when they were looking into him before she married him. It was from that day forward Francine kept her wifely status so pristine while behind the scenes wanting to get to Dexter's money.

What shocked Vanity the most was that Drexel was fulfilling his dead brother's wishes even though he wanted nothing to do with his family at that time. On top of that, Vanity was not even married to Dexter so what right did she have to his money anyway? Something was not making sense. Did Drexel know about the recent events that made Vanity believe that Dexter was still alive?

Drexel started, "Vanity, I know all of this is out of the blue but I want you to know that I talked to Dexter when you two had a good thing and I know that he would want me to see this through. My nieces and nephews, even the ones with Francine, need to know that their father left them something and he wants you to be responsible for making sure they are taken care of."

"Drexel, this is so much to take on." Vanity said for the umpteenth time.

"Well you leave tomorrow so when do you plan to tell me what you're going to do?"

"I have had time and it's a crazy thing of me to even think about but if there is something I need to do, to ensure you fulfill this mission for Dexter, I will do it. I do have one condition."

"What is that?"

"That you make that restaurant deal a reality. I will not be here doing nothing. I work. That's what I like to do and I don't care how much money he's left me, I need to be doing something that makes me happy."

"How long will you consider staying here?"

"It takes me about six months to get a new restaurant off the ground. I will commit to at least that much time."

"Thank you. I am happy to hear that. Will you bring your family?"

"Uh, no. I am not trying to make this a family reunion type of thing. I hope that is not what you're expecting?"

"No. I was not. I will have Wilma prepare your room."

"My room? I am not staying here with you."

"Please, this is our family estate. You are family. You gave birth to McKnight's and that means you are family."

"Oh, well I have not thought of it that way."

"So, you will stay?"

"Stay at the estate, yes. I do need to go back to the States to wrap up a few things before coming back here."

"I understand." Drexel said.

"Good. I will fly out tomorrow as scheduled and when I come back, I expect you to have a meeting set up for me. Otherwise, this deal is off."

"I can see what my brother seen in you. He said you were quite feisty."

"Oh, did he? Well, he was quite persistent himself; which is how we got into this mess in the first place. Speaking of which; where is your wife? I've been here for several days and I haven't seen the woman of the house."

"I'm single."

"Children?"

"No." He said with apprehension in his voice. It did not seem like a topic he wanted to talk about, especially since it was never brought up during any of their other conversations.

"Oh. Well, I guess I will have plenty of time to hear all about that when I return. I will not pry too much."

"Thanks."

Drexel started to relax, went over to the mini bar, and poured a glass of bourbon.

"Are you okay?" Vanity asked.

"Yes. I am sorry. I just don't like talking about that."

"Well, I think you know so much about my life but I don't know anything about you so I just asked."

"It's okay and I understand why you would ask. Should I call Clayton to usher you back to the hotel?"

"Yes. I should get packed."

"When can I expect you back?"

"I need a couple of weeks to get things in order."

"I look forward to seeing you again."

He came over and gave Vanity a genuine hug. He was built just like Dexter. He was firm and tall but his skin was much darker. After seeing him these past few days, Vanity could see the resemblance. After seeing the family photo albums, they were a split between their parents. Drexel took after their mother while Dexter took after their father who was much fairer skinned.

Clayton walked in during the embrace and cleared his throat. Vanity was startled and broke away from Drexel's arms as if it was wrong or like she was enjoying being close to the man who was part of the man she loved.

"Ms. Rodriguez, the car is here to take you back to Dunston Hall."

"Thank you Clayton, I will be right out."

"Very well." He walked away.

"Well, Drexel I will see you soon."

"I look forward to it."

Vanity walked away unsure about that last statement. She did not turn back to see if he was watching her walk away because if he were, she would not want to confirm that she felt him getting close to her.

On the way back to the hotel Clayton watched Vanity while he sat across from her in the limousine. "What did I walk in on?" Clayton finally asked.

"What are you talking about?"

"Are you getting close to Mr. McKnight?"

"What? Of course not."

"Good. It would not be a good idea."

"Excuse me? When the hell are you men going to stop trying to tell me what I should be doing with my damn life? Shit! This is getting very old." Vanity was pissed and she had just started to get over that feeling the past few days.

"Vanity, I am just warning you that things are not as they seem. Just be wise and if you're going to take Mr. McKnight up on this offer to come back to England, understand that you are doing it for Dexter."

"For Dexter? This is crazy! You all are crazy! Do you know that? Dexter is dead! And the last time I checked, he cannot come back from the dead and disapprove of who I involve myself with."

"I will not be back here in England to watch over you. You'll be on your own so I am just asking you to be careful."

"Well then just say that. You are always speaking in codes and I do not like that. I need you to talk straight."

"I do not know Drexel McKnight well so I am leaving you in his hands because I was able to confirm all of the things that Dexter asked of him."

"Oh really? When were you going to share this good bit of news?"

"It was not important once we got here. Drexel had already told you everything."

"The only reason I am coming back is because I want St. Christopher's to have a London location. Therefore, I am doing this out of selfish motives. I can care less about the money because more money more problems. I am fine with my status. I will be putting everything in accounts and trust funds for all the kids."

"I am sure you will do the right thing."

"I'll be damned if I let Francine's family run me away from my country trying to keep money from them. So this is not a permanent thing so let's get that straight right now."

"You'd be surprised how people live their lives trying to take from others."

"I don't live like that and I'm not about to start changing my life to protect an inheritance that isn't even mine. I will come back for about six months and after that, I will continue to move on. Besides, I have a wedding to plan."

"Grant." He said disappointedly.

"Yes, Grant. What makes you say his name like that?"

"Vanity, he can't know about any of this and if he's as protective as some men are, he will not want you to live in another country for six months and he cannot come visit."

"Why can't he visit?"

"You heard the stipulations. You cannot be with Grant right now. Drexel doesn't trust anyone."

"Then why the hell does he trust me?"

"Because Dexter trusted you."

"Damn him." She thought about Dexter.

Love on Fire

Emotions came over her and tears formed. She had not cried in months thinking about Dexter. This trip had stirred up so many emotions that it was only a matter of time before she would be filled up and the cup would run over.

Clayton came over to Vanity's side of the limo, wrapped his arm around her shoulder, and let her lean on him. "It's okay." He said trying to console her. It sounded weird coming from him but it was at least genuine.

Vanity cried the rest of the way back to the hotel. When they pulled into the driveway, she wiped her face and took a deep breath. The driver opened the door and Vanity exited followed by Clayton.

In her room, Vanity took her time packing her things. Somehow, she felt the presence of Dexter again. Was it being in England, where he was born? Was it his brother Drexel or was it all of the above? She did not quite know but for the first time in a long time, she wanted to wake up from this bad dream.

A long hot bath was definitely in order. The housekeeper put lavender on her pillow and she picked it up, inhaled the scent and then tossed it in the running water. She needed to exhale and take in the decision she made to move to England for a reason that she was still cloudy on. Taking care of the money was one thing but there had to be more and she felt like she would not find out the underlying cause of that until she was back and had more time to be around the McKnight family.

A warm hand found her nipple under her silk nightgown. It was a hand she recognized. From one to the other, the nipples hardened wanting more. She turned on her side and there he was. He laid there with a smile that he was pleased to see her. He pulled up her nightgown and took her breast into his mouth. He left them and found her lips that glistened from the night moon shining through the window. He kissed her deeply. She accepted and responded to his tongue as it explored all of her mouth. Tracing her full lips and kissing her sweet and sensually. She smelled him. It was a scent she recognized, loved and enjoyed. She took a deep breath and inhaled his scent. He ran his hand down her waist and hips. His left hand cupped her shaven pussy. He rubbed it and stroked her clit. He slipped his fingers farther to see if her pussy was as wet as it always gets when he came to play. It was. He grabbed her by the waist and pulled her into a riding position. His dick fit perfectly like no other could take its place. He took her hands in his and helped her ride his dick until they both came. She laid forward on his chest and took another breath to inhale him and his scent.

Vanity rolled over in her sleep and the bed it was cold and empty. She sat up in a pant as her body was still recovering from her wet dream.

five

Back in the States, Vanity decided to get her affairs in order as soon as she could. The last thing she needed was Cole trying to figure out why she was going back to England so soon without a business deal.

Grant was another story. The goal was to get into town and out before anyone other than her assistant Leslie would notice. The next couple of days, Vanity planned to lay low. There was business to finalize at the new location and that was it. A London location was coming online in six months. She had a lot of work to do and she needed to get her partners on board so she could get over there and make it happen.

"Ms. Rodriguez, I have a Mr. Clayton here to see you."

"Send him in." Vanity said.

Clayton entered Vanity's oversized executive office. He did not wear his usual black get up; this time he wore the most casual attire Vanity had ever seen. Something was up.

"Clayton, what is going on?"

"Yes, Ms. Rodriguez, I apologize for the unannounced visit. I wanted to tell you in person before anyone else got a chance to." He said with worry on his face.

"What, what is it?"

"The twins have been kidnapped."

"What!? When?" Vanity said grabbing the phone.

"No! Don't do that. Cole cannot talk to anyone or they have threatened to hurt them."

"They! Who is they?"

"We don't know yet." Clayton answered.

"We? Who is we?"

"Drexel and I."

"Drexel? How does he know so much already?"

"The ransom was sent to him."

"What the hell for? Who even knows that they are Dexter's children? That was a closed adoption."

"That is what we are trying to figure out. We think Francine's family is involved. Did she know you were pregnant?"

"I think so but it was never something we openly talked about." Vanity answered, thinking back on the altercation between her and Francine at the hotel years ago.

"It is obvious that someone knows. The twins were kidnapped from the elementary school."

"Oh, no. I need to get to Vegas."

"Vanity, wait. Please just calm down. We are doing everything we can do right now. Drexel has the FBI on it and we have to be patient."

"I can't just sit here and do nothing. My sister needs me."

"Vanity, you cannot make this bigger by showing up in Vegas. " Clayton tried to calm her.

"This is not happening. Those are my babies. What are we going to do?" Vanity sat in her chair, put her head in her hands, and just started to pray.

"That's all we can do right now." Clayton sounded comforting.

It felt like hours before Clayton received a phone call with an update. His contact with the FBI had explained that they had traced the call to a local warehouse in Vegas and were going to check it out.

"Vanity, let's go to your place. Waiting here is not going to be a good idea. Besides, I think you could use a drink to calm your nerves."

"Okay." Vanity did not say another word before she turned off her computer and started for the door. When she got to the threshold, she nearly knocked Grant over.

"Oh, Grant. You scared me. What are you doing here?"

"I guess, hi or how are you isn't in order?" Grant sounded dejected.

"I have an emergency situation and I need to get home." Vanity did not sympathize with him because all she could think about was her twins.

"Emergency? What's going on?"

Clayton interjected, "I'm sorry Grant, but she is not at liberty to discuss that with you?'

"Who the fuck are you? Vanity, who is this guy?" Grant flipped his thumb in Clayton's direction.

"Look Grant, please go. I will call you!" Vanity brushed by him toward the door.

"Vanity!" Grant yelled out.

Clayton turned back to Grant and put his hand up to his chest to hold him back, "Sir, please. Stand down. She said that she would call you."

"Get the hell out of my face." Grant brushed his hand away and rushed passed Clayton to get ahead but Clayton was too quick. He grabbed Grant by the arm and folded it behind his back.

"Aghh!" Grant moaned.

"Let her go." Clayton said between his teeth.

"Aight, man damn! Let go of my arm." Grant pleaded.

"Next time, I will not be so nice." Clayton let his arm go once he could see that Vanity had made it out of the parking lot. "Go home."

Grant did not say a word. He left the building, got into his truck, and sped off. Clayton hoped that he would go away quietly. The last thing they needed was Grant snooping around in these affairs.

When Vanity arrived at her home, things were different. She did not like the fact that people were after her and her family. What had she gotten herself into messing around with Dexter? This was starting to look like a scene in a movie. Money, kidnapping, criminals, and the feds – it all was a bit much for her to take on.

Before she could get in and take off her shoes, the doorbell was ringing. "All be damned." Vanity went to the door. It was Clayton.

"I told you I would be over. Don't look so surprised." He said stepping over the threshold.

"I am just on edge. This is too much. What has Dexter got me mixed up in? He is dead and still somehow is managing to cause havoc in my life."

"Now, hold on. Dexter did not have anything to do with this. I will not let you run his name through the mud like this."

"My life has been a mess since the day we reconnected. I have yet to get back to life as normal. And as soon as I attempt to move on, shit start happening."

"It's just bad timing."

"Bad timing! You've got to be joking!"

"I wish I was. I did not know all of this would happen either but I am just glad that I am around to help you. Had I not been here, who knows what trouble you'd find yourself in."

"Hey! I do not need you to take care of me. Let's get that straight right now."

"Yea, okay, Vanity."

"For your information, I was fine with Grant protecting me – he just doesn't know all of the shitty details and by now, I would have told him."

"Exactly, the problem. This is a sensitive situation and because it involves the Mansell family, it is above your beach boyfriend's head."

"You keep talking like that and you'll be standing on the other side of the door and you can keep watch from there, smart ass. And before you get too comfortable, it's Ms. Rodriguez to you."

"Very well. I digress."

"That's more like it. Now, do you want a drink or anything before I go to my room?"

"I'm fine. Thank you."

"I will be upstairs. If you need me, you will need to use the intercom over there." Vanity pointed to the intercom and made her way up to her room. She needed a shower to relax. The drink had not kicked in and she knew it was going to be a long night.

She heard Clayton dialing on his cellphone before she made it halfway up the stairs; which meant there should be some news about the warehouse soon.

Love on Fire

After the long shower, Vanity went to her home office and got on the computer to see if she had an email from her daughter Christina. Her mailbox had junk mail but nothing from Christina.

Staring back at the computer screen, Vanity was startled by the intercom blaring with Clayton's voice. "I need you to come down."

Vanity jumped up from the computer and ran down the staircase to see what he wanted. "Did they get the twins?"

"No. The warehouse was empty. They set up some remote phone system. It doesn't appear as if anyone was ever there."

"What?"

"I am waiting to hear back from them again because something was going down in the middle of the conversation."

"Something? Like what?"

"I don't know. I'm in the dark until they tell me our next move"

"Our next move?"

"Yes. I think we may end up in Vegas so you may want to pack a bag."

That was all she needed to hear. On her way up to her room, Vanity heard Clayton dialing on his phone again.

❤❤❤

When they landed at Carson International Airport, Vanity had the weirdest feeling in her stomach. She did not like the way her nerves were jittering and her heart was pounding the closer they got to the streets of Vegas.

"This way." Clayton directed Vanity toward the driver holding a sign with the name "Savannah."

Vanity chose not to question the name and just did what she was told. Inside the Lincoln Town car, there were three men. One sat in the front seat next to the driver, who stayed focused on what was in front, while the other man in the back focused on what was around the rear.

"Who are these people?" Vanity whispered.

"The agents working the case." Clayton responded.

"Where are we going?"

"To the case headquarters."

"What? Why? I want to see Cole and Christina."

"Vanity, please. I need you to cooperate. We will get to the bottom of this but you have to be patient."

"Patient, my ass. Those are my babies."

"I understand. That is why you have to let us handle it. You're too emotionally involved."

"Fine. I hope you know what you're doing." Vanity said in a lower tone. It was not a good idea to get upset. She would start watching and listening. It would start with Clayton. He knew something and he has not told her. She did not even know why they had to come to Vegas.

"Hello." Clayton said into his cellphone. He uttered a few words in agreement but that was all.

"When we get to headquarters, I do not want you to mention anything about the recent connection you made with Drexel or the future plans of returning to England. Understand?"

Vanity nodded.

The rest of the ride was dead silence. No one spoke. The familiar streets of Vegas and all of its glittering lights did not faze Vanity. The agents were also unaffected by all of the street traffic as they rode down the strip toward Downtown. They pulled up to the curb and Vanity looked around and did not see anything that looked like headquarters.

"We're stationed inside Five Kings Hotel." Clayton cleared her anxiety.

"Okay."

Vanity and Clayton walked toward the hotel and the agents remained in the car. When they reached the casino, Clayton grabbed Vanity's arm and placed it in his as a groom takes his bride. She immediately stiffened.

"Relax. It's just until we make it to the elevator."

When they arrived at one of the service elevators, he pressed the down button. When they got onto the old elevator, they went down toward the basement. Vanity had not been in this hotel in many years. She had tried to do business with them but they were not ready to spend the money it would take to renovate the hotel. From the looks of it, things have not changed since the last time she stepped foot in the hotel some fifteen years ago.

The basement smelled like any other basement. It was old. The walls were pale and the only people they saw were the hotel staff. They approached a door with a small square window. Clayton pressed the buzzer.

When they were inside the room, Vanity saw her daughter Christina and Cole. She rushed over to her daughter and hugged her tightly.

"Let me look at you." She grabbed her face and held her back at arm's length.

"Mom, I'm fine." Christina said.

"What happened to you?" Vanity questioned, not convinced.

"Nothing." Christina assured her.

"Ma'am, please come over here, we have some questions to ask you." A man in a suit interrupted her conversation with her daughter.

"Wait a damn minute. I just got here." Vanity snapped.

"Ma'am we don't have a lot of time." He replied.

"Vanity, please." Cole intervened.

Vanity left her daughter and followed the man to another part of the room. She looked around at a glance and the room looked like a security office. There were cameras all over the walls and pictures of patrons who were probably banned from the hotel for one scam or another.

"Ma'am, we have to get a ransom in order to have something to bargain with." The agent said.

"How much?"

"Twenty five million."

"Twenty five million dollars!?" Vanity snapped. "How do they know I have that kind of money?"

"We do not know but Drexel is willing to deal if you will participate. You are the only one he trusts. That is why you're here."

"What's the plan?" She said quickly.

Vanity did not think twice about the money. It was not hers anyway and if using it would get the twins home safely, she did not care if they asked for every red cent. This money from Dexter has been nothing but trouble and with every day, it was not getting any better.

The agent asked Vanity to get half of it wired to the account and the other half would be exchanged for the kids at the rendezvous point. Vanity thought she was in a twilight zone. This was not happening to her. The twins that she gave birth to had to be some type of royalty and she did not know it. Who would kidnap them knowing that they would get so much money for their safe return? She could only think of one person. Francine.

For the next couple of hours, Vanity and Cole sat close and waited.

"Where is Robert?" Vanity finally noticed that he was not there.

"He was not allowed to come. He's at home waiting and probably going out of his mind."

"But why?"

"They wanted him to be at home just in case something developed there."

"Cole, how did this happen at the school? Don't they have security?"

"Yes, they go to a private school and I don't know if a teacher knew who they were or what but we both know this adoption was closed and their name is not McKnight."

"So, you know this is about them being McKnight's, then don't you?"

"Of course. They told me that the kidnapper mentioned something about their name and that only meant they wanted money."

"I'm so sorry this is happening."

"It's not your fault. I just want my babies back."

"We will get them back." Vanity grabbed her friend in her arms and embraced her. "It's going to be fine."

The phone rang out loudly across the room.

"Show time!" The agent said.

Vanity stood up and was ready to go.

"Ma'am, not you."

"Like hell, not me! I'm going."

"Vanity, please do not make a scene. The agents are professionals and they do not want to give the kidnappers any more hostages. Please stand down." Clayton instructed.

"Clayton, please don't patronize me. If you're going, then I'm going. End of story."

Clayton sighed and did an about face and knew that Vanity would be on his heels.

"Cole, I'll be back." Vanity said. "With our babies."

Vanity did not know how in the hell she would keep that promise but she had to do what she needed to do to get the twins back and she could not trust anyone to come back with any crazy stories about how 'things went wrong'.

Cole was trying to keep it together but she was a pure mess and the last thing that Vanity wanted to do was sit around and wait. Since she was putting up the ransom, she was going to be there for the exchange.

The same agents from the airport drove in silence again, Clayton looked over at Vanity with steel eyes. He was angry but she did not care. He was not in charge and besides, he should have known that once she got involved that she would see it through.

"Don't look at me like that."

"Van...Ms. Rodriquez, this is dangerous and you're putting yourself in harm's way."

"Oh, please."

"If anything happens to you, it's my ass on the line."

"So that's what this is about?" Vanity snapped.

"I have to get you and the twins to England as soon as this is over."

"What? Excuse me? The twins are not going to England."

"I have to tell you about that later."

"Clayton, don't play games with me. We cannot uproot them from the only family that they know."

"It's not up for discussion right now." Clayton concluded.

"As soon as this is over, we need to have a serious discussion about how you and the rest of the world are planning my life."

The ride was longer than she expected. They ended up on Highway 10 in the desert. The sun was descending over the mountains to the west and the air was dry with a slight summer breeze. When they approached a gas station on the side of the road, there was a black van parked near the pump.

"When we pull up, you must stay in the car. We cannot let them know you are here." Clayton demanded.

Vanity did not respond but he knew she would comply.

The van had tinted windows and it was impossible to see who or how many people were inside. The agents parked across the road on the opposite side of the gas station to keep their eyes on the station, the road and the van. A cellular phone rang out and it startled Vanity.

"Yes. Step out of the vehicle, with the children." The agent directed the caller while looking at the suspects van.

Love on Fire

The van door opened and a tall muscular built man stepped out of the passenger seat. He was clean-shaven and wore a business suit. These were professionals, Vanity thought watching the scene intently. He looked over toward the agent's car before he slid the side door of the van open to reveal that the twins were unharmed.

"Stay in the car." Clayton directed as he and the agent gave each other the nod to exit the sedan.

The agent exited with the duffle bag of money in hand. Vanity was eyeing the entire scene with anxiety as she could now see the fear on the twins faces. That made her angry.

When the agent and Clayton stopped midway, the man turned to the children and said something and they climbed out of the van. Some words exchanged between the men; Vanity saw Collin go over to the agent and grab the duffle bag while Cassidy stayed with the kidnapper.

Once the kidnapper took the bag from Collin, there was a sound, "Pop! Pop!" The kidnapper hit the ground and the driver's body slouched over the steering wheel. Vanity turned her heard in time to see the agent in the front seat pull back his silencer pistol. The rest happened so quickly. Clayton grabbed the twins as quickly as he could while the other agent drew his weapon and pointed it at the van looking for others. Vanity opened the door to the sedan and stayed as low as possible waving the children to come to her.

Both kidnappers shot dead. The agent picked up the duffle bag from the ground and walked back to the car.

"What happened back there?" Vanity asked snuggling the twins closer to her.

"I don't know." Clayton said, still trying to catch his breath.

"Did we just ambush those men?" She asked.

"I had no idea that was their plan. It happened so fast." Clayton said now aware that the agents had just shot those men and left them for dead. Vanity sat in silence all the way back holding her twins close to her bosom.

six

When Vanity came through the door with the twins, Cole jumped up and ran over to them. Robert had come to wait with her and he was struck with happiness as his children walked through the door. Cassidy and Collin jumped into their parents arms. Cole wept and Robert enclosed them all in a protective hug. It brought tears to Vanity's eyes to see them reunited. This did not have to happen and before it was all over, she would get to the bottom of this drama. It started with Drexel. Vanity had to get back to England and get the truth behind all of this.

Clayton came over to Vanity and pulled her aside, "You need to find a way to tell Cole that we need to take the kids to England."

"Clayton, I will do no such thing. I am not taking the twins away from the only family that they know."

"They are not safe here."

"Why? What the hell is this about?"

"I am not at liberty to tell you that right now."

"You will need to tell me something because I am not taking them to England with me." Vanity said matter of fact.

"I will find out if we can put them in protective custody and get back with you."

"You do that. I do not expect anything less than what I am requesting. Cole has nothing to do with this and the children are even less involved. This is about me and these damn McKnight's and when I go to England, I am going to sever this tie once and for all."

Vanity walked away from Clayton to join Cole and her family who had started gathering their things to leave. Christina was right on their heels, who had become closer to Cole and the kids since Vanity had moved to California.

"Christina, I'm going to be staying at the Cosmopolitan tonight."

"Okay, can I crash with you?"

"Sure. Let me finish up here and we'll leave in about five minutes."

♥♥♥

The agents pulled into the hotel with Clayton, Vanity and her daughter, Christina in tow. The driver helped them with their overnight bags and took instructions from Clayton.

In the hotel lobby, Vanity had a flashback of her and Dexter on one of their many rendezvous. With all of the drama that had transpired in the last twenty-four hours, it left the possibility that Dexter was somehow still alive. She felt it.

After getting the room key, Vanity gave one to Christina. "Go ahead to the room. I'm going to get a drink from the bar before I go up."

"Mom, I'm over 21, I can go to the bar with you." She chuckled.

"Oh, sweetie, I did not mean it like that. Please join me if you'd like."

"Great. I could use a cocktail myself."

Vanity did not invite Clayton and she hoped he did not get offended but she had enough of him and all of his secrets for one day. A good catching up with Christina was just what the doctor ordered.

Vanity went to the bar with her daughter. Christina ordered her a top shelf martini and Vanity ordered the same.

"So, mom are you going to tell me what's going on?"

"Going on with what?"

"Please don't do that. The twins were just kidnapped for twenty-five million dollars and you're going to act like it's nothing going on."

"Honey, this is not the time or place to speak about that. Yes, there is something going on but I am in the dark as well."

"How? You're the one who they wanted."

"How do you know that?"

"I overheard the men talking before you arrived."

"What men?"

"The agents."

Vanity's blood started to boil. Clayton was keeping important details from her and she did not like that. What would these people want with her?

"Let's talk about something else. I have to speak to Clayton about this further. I promise to tell you what is going on so you are not worried. Okay?"

"Fine. How's Grant?"

"Oh, that's another topic for another day?"

"What? Why? Did you two break up?"

"Not necessarily. We're just not on the best of terms with all of this going on."

"Does he know what's going on? Does he know about Dexter at all?"

"Yes, he knows about Dexter but like the rest of us, he doesn't know what all of this is about."

"Mom, he's a great guy. You need to call and talk to him."

"I will Chris and thank you. You know me. I'm stubborn as a bull and I need to know what's going on or we could really be over and I don't want that to happen."

"Anyway, I talked to Dad yesterday. I had not heard from him in a while. He called to see how things were going."

"Oh, really? That is nice. I haven't spoken to your father in years."

"I know. It's okay. I tell the both of you how the other is doing so you don't have to ask. He's engaged."

"Oh."

Vanity thought how ironic was that.

"Yes, some woman he met at a university conference. She's a professor at another university in the Seattle area."

"Good for him. How about you? Are you dating?"

"I am seeing someone." Christina replied shyly.

"What's his name?" Vanity asked.

"Thomas. He went to Yale also. We were friends in college and he received a job offer in Vegas about six months ago."

"He came out here to be with you?"

"I guess you can say that."

"Is this serious?"

"Mom...what do you mean serious?"

"Are you in love?"

"Goodness! I said we are dating. He hasn't proposed if that's what you really meant."

"Well yeah. I think you're still so young and need to live your life before you settle down."

"Mom, believe me, I am focused on building my career and we're having fun together so whatever happens, happens."

"Alright, then cheers." Vanity raised her glass, tapped Christina's in a toast, and took a swig of her martini. Thoughts in her head about her daughter growing up, having sex and someday getting married were too much. She only hoped that Christina would find the right person the first time around and not end up like her.

After their cocktails, they left the bar only to see Clayton standing post outside the restaurant. Vanity did not even bother to speak; she whisked right by him and headed toward the elevator. Clayton noticed the cold shoulder but followed closely behind them anyway.

Inside the elevator, Vanity turned to Clayton with anger in her eyes, "We have to talk. Tonight." She concluded.

"Very well." He said.

When the elevator reached the floor, Clayton got off first to hold the door open for them and guided Vanity and Christina to their room.

"Chris, go ahead in. I need to speak to Clayton."

"Okay, mom."

When the door of the room closed, Vanity lead Clayton down the hall toward the elevator lobby where there was a window with a view of the city.

"Clayton, is there something you are not telling me about this situation?"

"Ms. Rodriguez, I have told you that there are things that you don't know for your own good. I am not trying to cause you any more discomfort by not telling you things but I am only..."

"Doing what you're told." Vanity finished his sentence.

"Right. Mr. McKnight is very concerned about you and the twins."

"Why? What is so special about them...us?"

"I am not sure but it has something to do with the family history of twin births. It's some kind of family tradition."

"What? That doesn't make any sense. I've never heard of such a thing." Vanity said in disbelief.

"Look, I am not here to convince you of anything. I'm just telling you that the twins have some type of insane inheritance."

"Why didn't Dexter ever mention any of this?" Vanity asked.

"I don't know. These are the things you need to ask Drexel when you go back to England." Clayton answered.

"I am not sure that I am going to be able to take the twins. This is all a little much and I cannot imagine Cole allowing it."

"Then I suggest you get started convincing her because he is not going to budge on this. He wants the twins in England." Clayton said matter of fact.

"I guess this is all I'm going to get for now." Vanity said.

"Sorry. I need to get to my room and get some sleep. Please stay in your room until morning. We still have this investigation going and until we know who is behind this we cannot take any chances."

"Okay. I will sit still for now but I am going back to LA by tomorrow night. I will talk to Cole in the morning."

"Good. Let me know if my persuasion will be needed." Clayton offered.

"No. I think I can handle it." Vanity said now back at her hotel room door.

"Good night, ma'am."

"Good night, Clayton."

Vanity closed the door behind her and went into the room to find Christina balled up in the bed and sleeping like a baby. It seemed like yesterday that she was just a baby and now she was a grown woman starting her own life. Vanity took a moment to enjoy watching her daughter sleep safely in her presence. The kidnapping of the twins was a reminder of how precious life is. She could not image what Cole went through when they went missing. A thought Vanity wanted to get out of her head quickly.

In that moment, Vanity picked up the phone and decided to call Drexel. In spite of what she was told, Vanity needed to make contact.

"Hello." Drexel's British accent came through the phone.

"Drexel, its Vanity."

"I know who it is. Why are you calling me?" He asked.

"You know what's going on here don't you?"

"Of course, I do. Are you and the kids okay?"

"Yes. Please tell me what is going on. I cannot be left in the dark like this."

"When are you coming back? We can talk then."

"No. I need to know something now. I am at the point where I feel like you McKnight's are running my life and I have no clue about what is going to happen from day to day. Is Dexter alive?" Vanity asked directly.

"Whaaat? What kind of question is that?"

"The reason that I need to ask you that is because this is getting a little weird and I have not built up the nerve to ask until now."

Vanity noticed an awkward silence and that only led her to believe that something was going on and Drexel was not saying. For some reason, Vanity decided not to pry. There was something going on and she probably would not find out until she went back to England.

"I think it will be best if you come to England. You are bringing my niece and nephew aren't you?"

"About that..." Vanity started.

"It's not permanent but I need you to bring them with you when you come this time. Please bring Nicole if you must."

"I will get back to you on that. They do not have passports yet. This could take time." Vanity explained.

"Okay but as soon as you can get it done, please get here. We have a lot more to discuss."

"Fine. I will see if we can get there in a couple weeks." Vanity said.

"Good." Drexel said.

seven

The weeks leading up to England, Vanity had to work on Nicole to get her to agree to take the trip. She eventually agreed because she wanted to know how to keep her babies safe. When they arrived at the McKnight estate Nicole's impression was flabbergasted.

"This is what Dexter came from? This is old money, girl. Look at this place." She said.

"I know. I had the same reaction when I first saw it."

The butler in the black and white uniform came to the car and helped escort the ladies and the children from the car. Drexel was right behind him smiling from ear to ear. He reached down to pick up his niece to greet her first.

"Hi, you must be Cassidy?" He gave her a hug and put her back down. Then he extended his hand for a shake to greet his nephew.

"And you must be Collin?"

Collin stuck his hand out reluctantly to shake the strange man's hand. "Hi," he said.

Nicole came over to her twins and took them each by the hand in a motherly way. She had no idea who this man was either. She had an idea but that did not mean anything after what they had been through.

"You must be Nicole." Drexel extended his hand.

"Yes and you are?" Nicole said in a tone that was not so pleasant.

"I am Drexel McKnight. Thank you for coming all of this way."

Vanity was finally making her way to the conversation when Drexel made that statement. "Well, I hope it is worth it. Nicole will not be here for six months."

Drexel looked puzzled but Vanity gave him the "not now" look. This was not the time to talk about that and besides, they had been on a long flight and she wanted to relax before they got down to business.

"Right this way." Drexel said. He led the family into the house and his service staff helped everyone to their room. When Vanity reached her room, the help opened the double door to a suite that looked like a scene from a movie. The bed sat on a pedestal that had to be at least two feet from the ground. The cherry wood sleigh bed was Victorian and the armoire and two nightstands on each side of the king sized bed were the only other pieces of furniture in the room. Exquisite paintings were on the walls. Vanity stood in the doorway breathless. This was not like the room she spent time in before. She was upgraded...but why? She thought.

"Ma'am, will there be anything else?" The staff asked.

"That will be all, thank you." Vanity went into the room and closed the door behind her. It looked like a master suite in the penthouse hotels she was accustomed to. The only difference was this was not a hotel. It was more intimate. It was more like a master bedroom in the home shared by a husband and wife. Immediately, something did not feel right.

Inside the master bathroom, Vanity found the walk in closet. It already had clothing, shoes, and women's accessories. "Whose closet is this?" She spoke aloud. Vanity looked at the tags on the clothing and everything was new. Shoes with soles that were new. Ironically, everything was her style and size. The brands she liked. The colors that complimented her. This could not be. She recalled the last time this happened back in Vegas when Dexter surprised her with the condominium when she was pregnant with the twins. He did the same thing. How would Drexel know all of this?

She made her way out of the bathroom, back to the main room to go downstairs and speak to Drexel to find out what was going on. The jet lagged feeling she had just moments ago was wiped away. When she opened the doors to head downstairs, Drexel was just approaching.

"Is everything OK in your room, Vanity?" he asked.

"Is everything OK?" Vanity repeated.

"Is there something wrong?" Drexel asked hearing the concern in her voice. He looked past her to see inside the room.

"Drexel what is going on? This room has clothing in it already."

"Oh, do you like them? I know you have so much business to conduct and I wanted to make sure you had everything you needed. My assistant did the shopping for you."

"Your assistant?"

"Yes, my assistant at my office. She did the shopping in Paris for me as soon as I knew you were returning. She had it shipped here just a few days ago." Drexel said.

"I brought my own things and besides, how do you know what I like?"

"You're a woman in business. It was not hard for her to make a few selections." He answered.

"Look, I am not sure what is going on here but I think we had better get down to it really fast. Something about this whole thing just isn't feeling right." Vanity said.

"Please calm yourself. There is plenty of time to do all of that. Your first meeting for the restaurant is in the morning. You may need some rest. Can I suggest a tea to relax you a bit?" Drexel genuinely offered.

"Fine." Vanity decided to fight this battle after the meeting. After all, her plan was to get St. Christopher's up and running within six months and she needed every minute of the next six months to do it. She gave Drexel a few kudos for scheduling the meeting so promptly.

♥♥♥

Over the next three months, Vanity and Nicole had become part of the McKnight family. Nicole had went back to the US at least three times to be with Robert and check on the business but she returned to be with her kids. The twins adjusted to the home schooling rather quickly. Nicole had more adjusting to do without her husband not being there. To keep herself busy she worked closely with Vanity on the restaurant. It was like old times. Her expertise was one that Vanity could never replace. They worked together like hand in glove.

"Nicole, now that we've set the opening date, I am going to let Drexel know that we have to make a move on the issue with the twins."

"What do you mean?"

"I have been quiet about it to this point but you need to get back to your husband and they need their father. Drexel has spent time with them and I don't want this to drag out any longer."

"What do you think you will find out?"

"I am not so sure anymore. At one point, I thought Dexter would pop out of nowhere and scare us all. Now, I am not so sure."

"I mean what happens with the twins. I mean their lineage is definitely the reason they are here, right?" Cole asked.

"See, that is what I was told before. I have not really put the pieces together on that and I think it's time we corner Drexel and get to the bottom of this."

"When?" Cole asked.

"No time like the present."

On the way down to the Drexel's office, Vanity gathered a few thoughts and choice words, just in case she had to use them. Whatever the twins had to do with them all being there had to come out now. Vanity wanted Cole to go back home to her husband and family where she belonged but she would stick it out until the end because she had other gains on the table.

At the door of the office, Vanity cleared her throat. Drexel looked up from the file he was reading.

"Please come in."

"I am sorry if we are interrupting. We need to talk."

"Oh. The universal woman's famous words." Drexel was not smiling.

"Yea, well. This has been put off with all of the movement going on with the restaurant but we need to get down to business regarding the twins. We've waited long enough."

"Very well." Drexel said and then got up from the chase and went to the bookshelf. He pulled out an old beat up book.

He sat down, opened the book, and for the next hour they listened to Drexel tell the history of the McKnight family. The Royal Family.

"Does this mean that my twins are royalty?" Vanity blurted before she realized that they were not her twins...they were Cole's.

"Yes. They are and the family secret regarding the affair of our mother and her fleeing back to the United States with Dexter created a disconnection with the family. He was the first born which would have made put him next in line to rule the dynasty of our family."

"Dexter is…was a King?" Vanity asked.

"By family tradition he was but when my mother fled the country, it changed everything." Drexel said shortly.

"Well then what is the all about? I am starting to get confused." Vanity was getting agitated trying to figure out how the twins fit into the picture.

"Dexter's death in the United States has been recorded and that leaves his children."

"He has children with Francine, though. What about them?"

"When Dexter told me about the twins, he changed the birth records regarding those children for some reason. When they were born, Dexter sent me copies of their birth certificates."

"Since I do not have any children, Collin is the next born son and that means that he has become next in line since my father, Pascal died a year ago."

Nicole was listening the entire time not able to say a word. The more she learned about this the more spaced out she became.

"Nicole, are you OK?" Drexel asked.

"Uh, I am not sure. The more I hear, the more I hear that my children belong to this family and not to me. I mean, how do I say, no to this?"

"I hope you do not. Life here is not so bad. The children can have the very best of everything. We want them to rejoin our family."

The bombshell. The McKnight's want the twins back in the family. No consideration or regard to the family who had become responsible for raising them.

"Wait a damn minute!" Vanity spoke up.

"What is it?" Drexel asked.

"You cannot be serious?"

"I am very serious. Dexter wanted this and I am only fulfilling his request to bring our family back together."

"Dexter is dead, gotdammit! Would you stop talking about him as if it really makes a difference? Those twins have been with Nicole and Robert since birth!"

"I know. Dexter should never have agreed to that knowing what he knew."

"It's too late for that!" Vanity shouted.

"You two, please stop." Nicole interjected.

They both looked at her and tuned in to her tone. She was not upset or angry; which surprised Vanity immediately.

"Cole, this is not going to happen. I am booking you and the kids a flight back to the US tomorrow. I've had it." Vanity stood up and walked toward the door.

"Wait..."

The voice that came from out of nowhere was not the voice of Drexel. The room was a dead silence. Vanity stopped dead in her tracks.

eight

FIVE YEARS EARLIER

"Dee, I need you to set something up for me." Dexter called from the secure mobile phone that Clayton brought to the hospital.

"What is it, big bro?" Drexel said in his British accent.

"The word is out that Francine has a contract out on me and I need you to take care of some details to get me out of the States."

"What? Where are you now?"

"I am in the hospital. They roughed me up a little bit but I am kind of glad it happened this way because my plan will work out even better."

"What plan?" Drexel asked.

Dexter always had an exit strategy if he ever ran into issues with Francine and her family. He did not know how they would make their move and when but it did not take long for them to decide after the affair and birth of twins to another woman. Going back to the UK was Dexter's only option to erase himself from the map. The only problem he had was leaving Vanity, the love of his life behind without as much as a goodbye. He would leave her and never return.

"Are you sure about this?" Drexel asked.

"Yes. Just do what I asked on that end and I will handle the rest. If I have never needed anything from my family, I need this. I cannot be the cause of death for Vanity or my kids."

"Consider it done." Drexel stated.

"Good. I will see you soon little brother."

The next day after the morning shift nurse left, Dexter made his move. It was only a matter of time before Francine and her mob cousins would show up to finish the job. He had to get out of the hospital undetected. The gift box delivered to his room contained a doctor's jacket and scrubs. With the strength he had built up, Dexter picked up his comatose roommate, who was a middle-aged man, and carried him to his bed only a few feet away. He slipped into the restroom, changed into the uniform, and within minutes was outside of the hospital undetected. The car Drexel arranged was waiting in the visitor parking area. When inside, the driver drove away. When they arrived at the airport, Dexter learned from Drexel that Vanity's car was bombed and her condition was unknown. Knowing he could not turn back Dexter's body went numb. His love and his everything may be dead. He could not make any calls or his plan would not work. Dexter had to leave the states immediately and not look back.

"Why?" He managed to whisper as tears burned his eyes.

At the security checkpoint, Dexter had managed to pull himself together and use the passport his brother managed to arrange for him.

"Mr. Johnathon Braxton, you are headed home, I see." The airport security said handing back the fake UK passport.

"Yes, mate. I am." Dexter tried to imitate a British accent.

Once through security, Dexter relaxed a little and made it to the gate where he sat still numb. He was going crazy not knowing what happened to Vanity. Is she okay? Did Francine do this? What was his next move? Dexter for once did not have any answers. He had no one to call. He was on his own until he reached London.

♥♥♥

Drexel was at the gate to greet his big brother upon his arrival. "You look a mess." Drexel said as soon Dexter walked up.

"Have you heard an update about Vanity?" Dexter ignored his brother's greeting.

"I did manage to find out that she is in critical condition but that was all. They are being very tight with information that even my connections are in the dark. They are investigating."

Walking toward the exit, Dexter had more questions for his brother.

"Did they say who is behind it?"

"The same who is behind the hospital bombing."

"What hospital bombing?"

"The hospital you were at. You are supposed to be dead now. The hospital room you were in was bombed and several people were killed and you were supposed to be one of them."

"Oh, shit. It was not supposed to happen like that. Got dammit!"

"What? What's wrong?"

"I could not go back to the US now, if I wanted to."

"Why?"

"They are going to consider me dead and the way I left the US, it will look like I faked my own death."

"Oh."

"Did you handle the affairs with the will and things as I requested?"

"I did."

"I just hope Vanity is alive to receive it."

"So what's the plan, bro?"

The twins, Dexter and Drexel were now together for the first time in their adult lives. It felt a little uncomfortable for them both but almost instantly they clicked and whatever anxiety they had disappeared before they made it to the McKnight estate.

❤❤❤

BACK TO PRESENT

"Dexter, is that you?"

From behind a closed door in the corner of Drexel's office, Dexter emerged. Vanity fainted.

❤❤❤

"Vanity, please wake up." Dexter's voice was soft and soothing. Vanity felt the energy and smelled the aroma of his cologne.

When she opened her eyes, they filled with tears. She had not spoken. She could not speak. This was not real. Dexter died in a hospital bombing five years ago.

"It is me. I am alive."

He said it but Vanity still could not move. Her mouth would not open to emit a sound. He rubbed her hair and put her loose strands behind her ear. That is when he kissed her lips.

The shock that sheered through her body awakened her all over. "Leave us." Dexter instructed Drexel and Nicole to leave the room.

Cole still in shock herself did not say a word and followed Dexter's command. Drexel closed the door behind them.

Dexter removed the engagement ring from Vanity's finger and placed it on the end table in Drexel's office. He kissed her ring finger as if reclaiming it. Vanity only watched as Dexter took control of her once again. She still had no words to speak.

"I am sorry baby for leaving you alone. I will never leave you alone again. Please say you'll forgive me." Dexter waited for Vanity to speak. She still could not.

He kissed her lips again. Her eyes were red from her tears and her body was still in shock. He scooped her up from the couch and took her to the door from which he came from. On the other side, it was living quarters. Dexter had been living there the entire time.

Vanity started to feel anger rise up inside of her. Her eyes opened wide and her body was awakening from its initial shock.

"You've been here this entire time?" Vanity finally said.

"Yes."

"You bastard!" Vanity wiggled from Dexter grasp and she slapped and beat on his chest. She yelled and cried obscenities all at once.

"I'm sorry...I'm sorry." Dexter stood there and took the blows like a punching bag. He knew he hurt her and that he deserved whatever he had coming to him.

"I need to get the hell out of here." Vanity ran for the door, back to Drexel's office.

Dexter tried running after her but he knew he had to let her go.

Vanity made her way through the office to the door. On the way, she stopped by the end table, picked up her diamond engagement ring from Grant, and placed it back on her finger.

"Cole!" Vanity yelled through the halls.

"Yes, Van." Cole came frantically from her bedroom.

"Pack your shit. We are leaving this house tonight and going to a hotel. I cannot stay here."

"Vanity what's going on?"

"The bastard is alive as you can see. I am furious and I cannot be here. I cannot see him."

"What about the restaurant?"

"He's alive now, he can finish it! I am going home. Get the twins packed. There is no way in hell we are staying and they can't make us."

"Okay. Okay. Please calm down you are scaring me. I will go pack our things right now." Nicole rushed off.

"Good. Be ready to go in 30 minutes. I will send for anything that gets left behind."

Vanity made it to her room and pulled out her luggage. She filled it with the things she brought from home. All of the clothing in the closet she still had not worn would remain. She did not want anything from Dexter or his family.

Waiting on Cole to finish packing, Vanity made reservations at a hotel near the airport and had their flights booked and set for an early morning flight.

When the cab arrived, Dexter called out to Vanity, "Vanity! Where do you think you're going?"

Vanity heard Dexter yelling from the bottom of the staircase but she did not respond. She was helping Cole get the twins baggage so they could leave.

"Vanity!" He yelled again.

By the time Vanity reached the staircase, Dexter was on his way up. "Don't you hear me calling you?"

"I hear you but I am not listening to you."

"Where do you think you are going at this hour?"

"Home."

"Home? To California?" Dexter asked bewildered.

"As a matter of fact, we have flights leaving in seven hours. We are going to a hotel for the night."

"But, why?"

Vanity gave a disgusting chuckle that she hoped answered his ridiculous question.

"Okay. Be mad at me but do not start making irrational decisions about this. You know there are still people trying to get to you and this family." Dexter explained.

"No, Dexter. They are trying to get to you. And if you do not put a stop to this soon, you will never see any of us again."

"What's that supposed to mean?" Dexter asked.

"It means that all of this planning time you've had I hope you came up with a plan to handle this shit because if not, we're going off the grid."

Dexter knew Vanity was right and he did have a plan but it did not include Vanity and the twins going back to the States. He had to let her go tonight but he had to try to put his plan in overdrive to ensure that they would be safe until he could sort everything out.

"Fine, Vanity. I will still be watching you and Cole until this is resolved. I hope you know that."

"Then I guess you'll get to see me and Grant fuck then." Vanity went for the uppercut.

"Vanity, that's not necessary." Cole intervened to break up their little spat.

"Well, I am just letting him know so he does not try to send his watch dog Clayton over to interrupt us this time."

"What do you mean this time?" Dexter interjected.

"Clayton was popping up at my place and had suspicions about you being alive. I see now that he was lying all along." Vanity said.

"Clayton did not know. No one but Drexel knew. Not even my mother knows." Dexter explained.

"Then why the hell was he watching me based on some instructions he said he was receiving? You know what...forget it. Let's go. I'm done with this conversation."

Vanity helped Cole with the kid's things before Dexter had a chance to say another word. Within minutes, they were in the taxi and headed out onto the main road. She did not look back but she knew Dexter was watching. Her heart was hurting. It felt like she was being stabbed repeatedly. She did not know which emotion to respond to now that she was out of his sight. Anger was on top but that is not what she really felt. She was disappointed and hurt. Crying would make it worse and she had to keep it together.

"Are you okay?" Cole asked.

"I will be. This has changed the game. I'm pissed."

nine

Vanity pulled into her driveway and to her surprise, Grant's truck was there. As much as she was mad at Dexter, dealing Grant was not the first thing she wanted to do. Explaining what had been going on over the past couple of months was also not on the list of things to do.

When Vanity hit the garage door opener to pull into the garage, Grant came out of the door with a box in his hand. He looked shocked to see Vanity, as he should. He had not spoken to her in weeks and he surely had no idea she would be back so soon according to her plan.

"What are you doing here?" Vanity asked closing the car door.

"What does it look like I'm doing?" Grant said coldly as he walked on the other side of the car to bypass Vanity.

"Where are you going?" Vanity called after him.

"The engagement is off Vanity. I am done with you and this mystery life you're living." Grant said putting his box in the bed of his pickup.

"Wait. I need to talk to you." Vanity walked toward the truck as he revved it up.

Grant did not even look Vanity in the eye before he put the truck in reverse and punched the pedal leaving the driveway.

Vanity stood there alone. What did she expect anyway? She was too late. Grant had had enough and he was not waiting any longer. Vanity retreated into the house not sure how to feel about Grant.

Her thoughts went to Dexter who would know soon enough that Grant was moving on. Vanity had to get herself together. She felt lost. Everything around her was out of order. Dexter had come into her life so many years ago and disrupted the flow of her life. Now look at her? As alone as ever. Not even her best friend was around to talk to.

Inside the house, Vanity noticed that Grant left a note:

Dear Vanity,

I hope that when you return that you have all of this figured out. I am sorry but I could not wait for you to do that. I tried to give you the space you needed but I have needs and I cannot do this anymore.

I am taking a coastal job with my uncle and I leave in two days. I will drop off your key at your office.

Keep the ring as a reminder of my love.

Vanity stood in the kitchen with the note and tears started to flow. He was gone.

❤ ❤ ❤

Back in London, Dexter and his brother had to pick up the pace on putting a stop to Francine and her attempt to destroy their family. After Vanity left, Dexter was even more afraid that she would do something stupid just because she was mad at him.

The brothers were in the study trying to figure out what their next move would be. "Dex, are you going to go back to the States?" Drexel asked.

"I want to but it's going to be hard. I vowed to never step foot back into that country but Vanity is making it very hard. I would never forgive myself if something else happened to her. "

"I know. So what are you going to do?"

"I may need you to handle this for me."

"Me?"

"Yes. I cannot go. You are the only one I can depend on."

"Dexter, you know how I feel about the US. I don't know..." Drexel was hesitant to agree.

Dexter did not want to push his brother but he needed him to agree. "I know, but she is the one. I told you that. I need her back...here with us."

"Us? Why? She is not my woman and really not yours either." Drexel said.

"Hey...what's with that? Are you jealous?"

"Jealous? Oh, no. I am not jealous. You have put this family through enough with this woman and those children. I was with you on this until now. This is on you. Now that your secret is out...you're on your own." Drexel stood up and left the study.

Dexter wanted to be mad at his brother but he could not. This was his problem. It always was. He brought his brother into this but it was time he put things back in order and go after what was his.

Dexter woke up with his sheets wet for the first time in months. It was all too familiar when he first left Vanity. After a while, he started focusing on watching and taking care of her and the feelings subsided but seeing her had stirred up emotions he had not felt in years.

♥♥♥

"Sir, passport please." The US customs agent asked.

Dexter had figured that the only way he could get back to Vanity was to create an identity and sneak back in. After Drexel decided he wanted nothing to do with the plan, Dexter had no choice but to get on a plane and go back to the United States.

It took a couple of weeks to finalize the plan, but Dexter was on his way back to the United States to handle his business with Francine and her family.

In the time that Vanity had been gone, Dexter found out that Grant had moved to the Caribbean, had left Vanity and the wedding was off.

Vanity had also fallen into a bout of depression. She was not working and the restaurant plans in London had fallen to the wayside. It was up to Dexter to get his life and Vanity's life back.

He had a plan. He had to get to Francine and her family without detection and all of those who were involved. Especially those involved with the kidnapping of the twins. Once he was able to get rid of the trouble they had caused, his ultimate plan was to make Vanity happy. If she did not want to move to London, Dexter would have to accept that and consider staying in the US. He wanted to be with her and be part of raising his twins. He never wanted to give them up for adoption but it was too late to take them from Nicole and Robert. That only left the option for him to stay in the US. He just did not know how he would do it.

Clayton made all of the arrangements for Dexter under his assumed identity. Dexter wanted to be close to Vanity so Clayton booked him in San Francisco. His plan to handle Francine would come later; he wanted to settle in and assess everything before making any moves and he wanted to do that as close to Vanity as possible.

The first night at the hotel, all Dexter wanted to do was be with Vanity, but he knew that it was no time for that because he still had work to do. He had to remain in the shadows of everyone until he could implement the plan. He also needed the children with Francine out of harm's way. Although they were grown and living on their own, they still believed, their father was dead. On top of all that, for the sake of his freedom, no one could know he was alive. He had to play it safe, be cool and wait on the perfect opportunity.

It had been weeks since Vanity left London and her emotions were all over the place. She was angry and alone and she did not know what to do. She tried everything to get her mind off Dexter and Grant but all she could think about was the two men that she loved and one of them put her in this crazy position.

Now, with all of this coming at her at once, Vanity did not know what to do. She wanted Dexter badly, she wanted his sex, she wanted his heart and to feel his affection but she knew that being with him would give him all of the satisfaction that he could leave her and come back into her life when he was ready. She could not give him that!

Vanity needed a bounce back plan. She needed to get back to London and finish the restaurant. She only had six weeks left to promote and get her staff and entertainers hired for the opening night. Dexter and his intentions would not get in the way of all the work she put into St. Christopher's.

"Leslie, please come into my office. We have some details to iron out for London." Vanity spoke into the intercom. Within moments, Leslie was in Vanity's office taking notes.

"Book my flight for next week. I'll need to stay closer to the restaurant this time."

"Yes, ma'am."

"The key that Grant left, can you use it to keep an eye on my place this time while I'm gone? I had a ton of mail last time and the post office left me a note about it."

"Sure. I go that way a few times a week after class." Leslie said.

"Thanks."

The rest of the afternoon Vanity was reviewing resumes. In pockets of time, she would drift off and think about the moment she heard Dexter's voice. She was starting to adjust to knowing he was alive and the anger she felt was subsiding. When she realized she was starting to forgive him, she would snap out of the daze and refocus on her work. Work was literally the only thing that kept her mind off him.

❤❤❤

"Hello." Francine said from her cellphone.

"Hi, Fran." Dexter said.

"What is this, some sick joke?"

"Trust me. It is no joke."

"Then why do you sound like my deceased husband?"

"Come 'on Francine. You know better. We need to talk and I mean privately."

"Meet with you? Are you freaking kidding?"

"Look, I know what you want."

"Do you? Now what is that exactly?"

"Money. That's what you've always wanted, my money."

"As usual, you don't get it."

"If it's not money that you want, then what is it?"

"I want your blood."

"Blood. You have done enough damage. What's wrong with you?"

Francine let out a devious chuckle, "There's nothing wrong with me. I see you're trying to save that bitch and her kids by trying to buy me off."

"Do you really want to spend the rest of your life in prison?"

"Who says I'm going after their blood."

"Francine, look…I'm not going to do this with you. I am going to give you that twenty five million you wanted when you had my twins kidnapped."

"The price went up. My cousin Vance was killed by the fucking FBI."

"I had nothing to do with that."

"It's fifty million now."

"Fifty?"

"You heard me. If you don't come up with fifty, I'll have the feds all over your Machiavelli ass!"

"Alright, alright. I will call you in a few days with the drop location."

"I will give you two days. On day three, I'll have the feds tracking your ass."

"Don't push me, Fran. I am trying to end this quietly but I will not hesitate to do what I have to do if you try any more bullshit."

"Is that so?"

"You're not the only one with ruthless connections. Remember, it's my money you want and it's the same money that can buy off anyone, including the Feds."

Dexter was only bluffing about the buying off the Feds part but she did not know that. After their negotiation, Dexter had to tell Drexel about the money. Drexel did not like the increase in funds but if it meant getting all of their lives back to normal, then money could not be an issue.

While Drexel worked on getting the funds together, Dexter decided he would ride by Vanity's place. He needed to see her.

When he pulled into the driveway, he could not tell if she was there but he was going to try anyway. He rang the doorbell and waited for a response. Nothing. He looked at his watch, figured that she was usually off work by this time, and should be there. He tried again. Nothing.

Retreating from the porch, he saw a black sports car approaching, it was Vanity. From the look in her eyes, he knew she was not happy to see him.

The garage door opened as she approached it and she pulled in. She barely came to a complete stop before she opened the door, "What are you doing here?"

"I wanted to see you. To talk. Will you listen to me, please?"

"I've had over five years to listen but you weren't talking then. What is so important that you have to talk about it now?"

"Please, can we go inside?"

"Dexter, you have some nerve coming to my place and expecting to just waltz right in."

"It's not like that. I know I owe you an explanation but you left London so quickly, I did not get a chance."

"I was not in the right frame of mind to listen to it then and I am not so sure I am ready now. You were dead. You did not exist anymore. Remember? How does one just openly accept that?"

"Van, let's please go inside. If after I explain what happen, you do not want anything more to do with me, then I will leave and never return. I promise."

"I'll give you five minutes."

Vanity opened the door and disarmed her alarm when she walked in. Dexter was right on her heels. He pressed the button to close the garage door before he crossed the threshold.

"Would you like something to drink?" Vanity asked as she went to the refrigerator for a bottled water.

"No...no thank you."

"Fine. Let's go into the living room." Vanity led the way.

"So, what's the story?"

"OK...well back when Francine and I got married, things were not what they seemed." Dexter started.

For the next fifteen minutes, Vanity heard a more detailed version of the story than what Drexel told. Drexel did not know all of the details about Francine and her devious ways. The biggest shock was that none of their three children was his biological children. She had several affairs that Dexter found out about but never told his children. For all they knew, he was their father and he wanted to keep it that way. Dexter performed paternity tests without their knowledge and when Francine found out about it, she always threatened to tell the children to spite Dexter.

"Once I found out she had been unfaithful for so many years, when the children were older, I told her I did not want any children with her. She was angry. Then you and I connected and you got pregnant...things between us happened so fast. I wanted to keep it a secret as long as I could because I knew she would try to hurt you. I knew the twins were royalty the moment you told me you were pregnant. That is why I reluctantly agreed to the adoption but I knew if I refused the adoption that Francine would find out and I could not take that chance."

"Dexter..."

"Wait...I'm not finished. Once I found out that we were in danger, I had to change the course of it all to get the focus away from you and me. Leaving was my only choice. I left hoping to save you, Cassidy and Collin."

"You did not trust me to know all of this. Why?"

"Vanity, you were in the hospital for weeks, I could not take a chance. Once you got out of the hospital you went to Puerto Rico and I just wanted you to start over."

"Then why come out of hiding now? Why are you doing this when I am moving on? This isn't fair."

"I love you. I love my kids and I want to be in their lives. I have always loved you and I could not allow you to marry someone knowing that I was still alive."

Vanity stood up, she became angry.

"So, you're admitting to interfering with my love life for your own selfish reasons!"

Dexter stood too.

"Yes." Dexter grabbed Vanity by the shoulders, "I do not want you to marry Grant. Ever."

"Get out of my house!" Vanity yelled, "Get out!"

Dexter let go of Vanity's shoulders and did not try to defend his statement. He had to let all of what he said sink into Vanity. The last thing he needed was to force himself upon her. He had to let her come to him, if she still loved him.

Vanity walked over to the door and opened it wide enough for Dexter to walk out.

"I'll see you in my dreams." He said and left.

Vanity knew all too well, what that meant. She would see him, too. Ever since he kissed her in London, her body would tingle at the thought. Her mind kept her angry and rejecting the feelings. Once she gave into the feeling, it would be over and she was not ready to let him win like that. She still had things to sort out. Then there is Grant. He left but she still missed him and the life they started to build together. Now that Dexter was back, she realized how much chaos he had stirred up in her life. Grant was drama free on all ends. She let a perfectly good man walk out of her life. He was fun, he was ambitious and his sex was more than satisfying. Dexter's magnetism had her so twisted and confused.

Vanity retreated to her room. She was not in the mood to eat. She turned on her favorite station from her cell phone and plugged it into the surround sound. The air filled with instruments and soft lyrics to calm the room.

After a warm bath, Vanity spent a little money shopping online. There were a few things to buy before the trip back to London. Her grand opening outfit. Something white. Her new signature color. Quickly Vanity was able to focus on her...at least until she went to sleep.

❤ ❤ ❤

"Clayton, are you ready for this transaction?"

"Yes. I have the schematics of the building and will have my men in place at 3 o'clock."

"Perfect. This time make sure there are no dead bodies." Dexter commanded.

"Yes, sir."

"I mean it, Clayton. That last exchange was not how it was supposed to go down. She blames me for her cousin's murder, you know."

"What? How?"

"Hey, let's not worry about that right now and get this shit done."

"I'm on it."

"Let me know when it's done."

Love on Fire

Francine would find out when the drop was made that Dexter would not be there. He could not take a chance that she would call the cops. He had a few people in his back pocket but he was tired of dishing out cash for his cover up. Besides that, he did not want to give her the satisfaction of seeing his face as he handed her the pay off. Giving her the money was not the point of this for Dexter anyway. This was a power move to get her off his back and out of his life.

Vanity landed in London and hit the ground running. She had interviews scheduled for the next two weeks with staff and entertainers. Vanity assumed that Dexter was still in California because she had not seen or heard from him since the week before when she practically threw him out of her house.

"Hello?" Vanity answered her cell phone.

"Hi, Vanity. It's Drexel."

"I know who this is. How can I help you?"

"I know you probably do not want to speak to me but I really am only offering my help. I understand you're back in London."

"I mean...I just got here today. How do you know this already?"

"That's not the point. Let me know if you need anything. You have my number." Drexel offered.

"Well, thank you but I think I'll be fine."

Vanity did not wait around for chitchat. She hung up the phone. Drexel was not on her good list either at this point. For what it's worth, at least he knew she was in London and she did not feel as alone.

❤❤❤

"It's done."

"Did you get the video?"

"I have everything. When do you want to me to deliver it?" Clayton asked.

"I will meet you and we can exchange. I have a little something for you."

"I will be leaving LA and heading east for a while after this. My flight leaves at 20:00 hours."

"I will meet in Vegas and we'll part ways then."

Dexter checked out of the hotel and headed to the airport. There was no need to stop by Vanity's because he knew she was in London.

❤❤❤

In Vegas, Dexter met Clayton to get the video coverage of the exchange. Dexter needed some insurance to show in the event it ever came back to bite him that he paid Francine off for her silence.

"Clayton, you've been a good man but I have to cut ties with you, man."

"What? Why?"

"It's time for us to put some years between us. No more business. I've had you working for me for the past 20 plus years and it's time for me to let you move on."

"When I meant I was going east, I did not mean to stop working for you."

"I know. I appreciate everything but I need to cut ties and get my ass back overseas before someone catches on to me being here."

"I feel you man. Well, if you need me, you know how to contact me."

"Likewise, my brother."

The two men shook hands before parting ways. When Dexter and Clayton walked away from each other, they did not look back. Dexter had given Clayton an envelope with information about his final payment and the account he sent it to. Clayton gave Dexter the copy of the video exchange with Francine and the key to the safe deposit box in Vegas that held the other copy of the video. Dexter did not plan ever see Clayton again.

♥♥♥

"Knock, knock."

"Dexter, what are you doing here?" Vanity asked.

"Can I come in?" Dexter was peeking his head into the office door.

"What do you want?" Vanity said not looking up from her paperwork.

Dexter came in to the office and closed the door behind him. "I wanted to tell you about Francine."

"What about that bitch?"

"I've handled it. She's out of our lives."

"Our lives? You mean yours?"

Dexter came around the desk and sat on the corner of the desk looking out the window, "I want you to accept my apology." He looked down at her.

Vanity still refused to look up at him. Dexter pulled up her chin to look at him. "I need you to forgive me." Dexter repeated.

"Dexter, it's not that simple."

"Can we at least start over?

"From what point exactly?" Vanity smirked.

"Can we at least just start by talking? How is the grand opening coming along?"

Vanity exhaled. She tried to be angry with Dexter but truly, she had to accept that he was alive. She never stopped loving him. The longer she tried to be upset and ignore the feelings the worse it felt. The love of her life was sitting inches away from her and she just could not accept it.

"It's going fine. I am interviewing for the grand opening during these next couple of weeks and after that I'll be arranging the marketing and special invites."

"Sounds like you are on track."

"Of course, I am. Are you going to make small talk or is there something else you want?"

"Vanity, please, be nice."

Vanity chuckled and did not say anything more. Vanity knew that if she did not find humor in the situation that would drive herself insane.

"Dexter, I will be cordial. Thank you for the visit. Was there anything else you needed?"

"Yes..." Dexter answered and leaned down and placed a sensual kiss on Vanity's lips. Before she could respond to reject the kiss, she was already accepting it. Dexter's tongue went deep. He placed his hand behind her head and toyed with her hair as he kissed Vanity deeper. She exhaled but did not stop kissing him. Dexter pulled Vanity to her feet and guided her in front of him.

"I've missed you my love...so much." Dexter said.

"I've missed you..." Vanity could barely get it out before she began to sob. Dexter stopped kissing

Vanity and took her into his arms. She was sobbing uncontrollably.

"I'm sorry...I'm so sorry." Dexter kept repeating.

The small corner office inside the complex for her makeshift headquarters became a sexual sanctuary for hours after his apology.

Dexter went up her skirt and pulled down her bikini panties. The room heated up and Vanity could feel her pussy pulsating like it had a heartbeat of its own. His hands gently cupped Vanity's whole pussy and he slipped his middle finger into her wetness to remind himself of what she felt like. "You're so wet." Dexter sat Vanity up on the desk and got down on bended knee. He wanted to be face to face with her pussy. He wanted to lick the inside of her thigh and have her call out his name...he knew exactly how to get her to do that. He slipped her panties completely off and spread open her thighs, his tongue gently massaged her clit and sensual moons escaped Vanity's lips. Dexter teased and toyed with her pussy and he claimed it just like their first time. She grabbed his head as he landed exactly where she wanted him to, "I'm coming...." Vanity let out an explosively wet orgasm that squirted all over Dexter's face.

"Vanity....that was..." Dexter could not finish his statement. He just wanted to get his dick inside her and feel her wrap herself around him. He stood up in front of her. Vanity wrapped her hands around his waist as his dick found its way into her. "It's been five years since..." Dexter words and voice faded as he closed his eyes and smiled at the sight before him. His love and his life was in his arms once again. His stamina was weak but he did not care. He came inside Vanity like a teenage boy on his first night. "Aaaghhhh!"

Dexter kissed Vanity on the lips, "Do you forgive me?"

"I don't want to talk about the past right now." Vanity placed her index finger over his lips.

Dexter sat in the desk chair with his pants at his ankles and sat Vanity on his lap. He wanted more and so did she. They did not talk, they just fucked as if he had been away on a long trip and they had both saved themselves for this very moment. Vanity rode Dexter's dick sensually and slowly. She knew just how to rub her click on his stubble happy trail to reach her plateau. His hands on her shapely hips guided her up and down on his thick dick. "Are you ready for me?" Dexter nodded in agreement and a few slow strokes and Vanity's creamy cum covered Dexter's shaft.

They went from one position to another, from one piece of furniture to another until they were exhausted. Making up for lost time was an understatement. They made love then they fucked and then they made love again. It was all in the movements and the moments. Dexter gave her the love that could only come from him.

Just like that, he was back into her heart as if no time has lapsed. Now, what was she going to do? Unfortunately, she had not thought that far.

Back at the McKnight Estate, Drexel was working out details with their attorney to cover the fifty million dollars that they had to send to America.

"Dexter and I will work this out. Don't you worry."

Dexter walked into the office in a panic to find out what his brother's urgent message was about. "What's going on?" Dexter asked looking over at their attorney.

"Well, it appears that Mrs. Francine tried to go spend a boat load of cash at once and has drawn attention to herself." Mansfield stated.

"What the hell does that have to do with us?" Dexter asked looking at his brother and then Mansfield.

"Well, a lot. She told them it came from you." Mansfield answered.

"What the hell? She has no proof of that. We made sure it was untraceable. Didn't we?" Dexter looked at Mansfield.

"Of course, I did what I had to do to launder the money for her; however, it is the name dropping and such that has drawn attention."

"What do you mean, name dropping? I used an alias."

"Exactly. The only three people who know you had an alias is me, Drexel and Clayton." Mansfield said.

"Well, I am sure as hell not going to think that Clayton ratted me out. There has to be some other explanation."

"What other explanation is there?" Mansfield asked.

"Clayton would not do that."

"We've tried calling him but his numbers are disconnected. He is off the grid." Mansfield said.

Dexter balled up his fist thinking about his last moment with Clayton when he severed their ties. He knew that Clayton would go so far under the radar that no one would find him. He did not want to dig into his old repertoire to find him; but he may have to.

"What do we do now?" Dexter asked to keep them in the dark about his plan to find Clayton.

"That's why I am here. We need you to lay low again until we can throw off the authorities who have started looking in to the alias we created. We know the lead will end up at a dead end but just in case we need to cooperate."

"Dexter, they may come to the estate to verify that you're not here." Drexel stated.

"What?" Dexter could not believe what was happening.

"Where's Vanity?" Drexel asked.

"She's at the office. Why?" Dexter questioned with worry.

"She needs to know this because they may try to question her and she needs to know what story to tell." Mansfield answered.

"I will call her." Dexter said going to the office phone.

Dexter made the call to Vanity and she was not happy about the interruption and especially that more drama had stirred up. She hated the drama and it seemed that as soon as it calmed down, more was sure to come. Francine had become a permanent thorn in her side. She had to figure out how to get rid of it because the men who were supposed to be in charge kept botching up the job.

Vanity eventually arrived at the McKnight Estate and learned of the details about the issue at hand. "Dexter, you and Clayton go way back. I am not sure this is true. I mean why would he do that?"

"I don't know but I am going to find out." Dexter said.

"How? You don't know where he is."

"I can find him...if no one else can." Dexter said.

Love on Fire

"But what about Francine? I thought this was over. I am losing my confidence in you men around here handling this shit." Vanity was sassy and frustrated.

"Calm down and stop with the foul language. It's going to get handled." Dexter said.

"That's what you said just hours ago. Now you are telling me it is going to be handled. Which is it?"

"Look, I need you to cooperate and just stick to the story if you get questioned. Nothing may become of their inquiries but we all need to be prepared."

"What does this mean for us? How long do you have to go back into hiding?" Vanity hated even admitting that.

"Just until we know the heat on their investigation is cooled off. I cannot make any moves until then. In the meantime, I want you to move into the house."

"Dexter, I don't know about that." Vanity was reluctant to agree.

"Come 'on Vanity. Please do not fight me on this. I want to make sure you are safe. Besides, you can stay up in your room."

"Okay, but it is only until the grand opening and then I am moving back to San Francisco."

"We can talk about that later." Dexter did not even want to think about Vanity leaving him again. For now, he would settle for her being in the same house where he could be sure she was safe.

"I'll send Max over to your hotel for your things." Dexter said.

"I need to go back to the office anyway, I can handle it. Besides, I want to check out the right way to lower any other suspicions."

"Fine. I'll drive you."

"Dexter, you cannot drive me. I'll have Drexel take me."

"Fine." Dexter did not like that either but he had no choice. He was stuck in the house again, for who knew how long.

Vanity made her way back to the office to pick up a few documents and then to the hotel. On the way, Drexel was quiet and did not speak a word but on the way back, he broke his silence.

"Vanity, you know that my brother is very mixed up in this mess with Francine."

"I do know this Drexel." Vanity gave him a "do I look like I'm stupid" look.

"He's gotten himself and this family in some deep trouble and I am just a bit fed up with it." Drexel admitted.

"What are you saying?"

"I am just saying that Dexter needs to fix this once and for all. This Francine woman is bringing attention to the McKnight name. We have to protect our legacy here in the UK and she needs to be stopped."

"What are you saying to me Drexel?"

"I am saying that this Francine woman needs to be dealt with. If Dexter isn't willing to do it, then I'm going to have to."

"Wait...why are you confessing this to me? What do I have to do with this?"

"I will need your help. Dexter is not able to carry out this plan. I need you to do it. You're the only one who can go back to the US and even have a chance of getting close to her."

"Wait a minute. You want me to kill someone?"

"To put it frankly, yes."

Vanity was flabbergasted, "What?"

"The only way to get rid of this type of person is to get rid of them. Are you going to be able to handle this or not, Vanity?"

"Well, wait a damn minute. You cannot just ask me to kill someone and expect me to agree. I will do no such thing. I can't stand that bitch but I am not a murderer."

"Fine. I will have to handle this myself." Drexel was irritated with Vanity but she did not care. Things were getting out of control and if anything, Vanity needed to calm them down...not go on a killing spree. Drexel was losing it, if he thought she would even consider such a thing.

"I assume I should not tell Dexter of your plan when we get back to the estate."

"You have assumed right."

Vanity planned to tell Dexter anyway but she wanted to know Drexel's angle. Why was he trying to do this in secret? It should be a plan that they both carried out. Something was not adding up and the last thing she needed was for Dexter to get side swiped with information that she knew all along. She was not like them.

When they arrived back at the house, the authorities were there. Drexel sat up straight in his seat and unbuckled his seatbelt before the car came to a stop. When he got out of the car, the authorities exited their car as well.

"Can I help you officers?" Drexel asked.

"Yes, Mr. McKnight we're here following up on some information we received about your brother Dexter being involved in identity fraud. Do you know anything about that?"

"Sir, my brother Dexter has been decease for over five years. What is this about? Vanity, you can go on inside while I talk to the officers." Drexel gave her a nod. Vanity obliged.

"Our records show the same but we received a tip that he was seen traveling on a European passport under the name Nigel Bobbin. Would you know anything about that?"

"Sir, this is absurd. I think you have received incorrect information. I would love to help you, but I can't."

"Mr. McKnight, here is my card. If you hear anything, please give us a call." The officer and his partner got back into their cruiser and drove away. Drexel waited until they were completely off the property before going into the house.

"Drexel, what did they ask?" Dexter said coming from the study.

"They know your alias alright. You are going to need a new one if you ever plan to leave this house again and you will need to start disguising yourself. If this doesn't cool down soon, they may always be looking for you."

"I'm not wearing a damn disguise!" Dexter yelled.

"You're going to have to do something or you're going to bring too much attention to this family...more than you already have."

"What's that supposed to mean?"

"Just what I said. You and this woman have caused so much upheaval that we are going to be the laughing stock of this town. If it weren't for Cassidy and Collin, I would have cut you off a long time ago."

"So, now you're telling me how you really feel."

"Yea...I have been..." Drexel started.

"Look you two...stop it. We have too much to do and this bickering is a waste of time." Vanity said.

The two brothers did not say a word. Drexel left the room and Dexter stood there with embarrassment on his face. "I'm so sorry. I feel like

I have ruined your life and everyone else's around me."

Vanity could not believe what she was witnessing. Dexter was getting emotional. "What is it?" she asked.

"I thought that coming home would give me a new start but I keep getting pulled backward. I know Karma is a bitch but damn...I need my life back. I need you back."

Vanity went over to Dexter and stood close enough to his chest that she could see his heart beating through his polo shirt. She wanted to hug him and tell him everything would be all right but she could not. Dexter needed to fix this for himself. She did not want to give him false hope about them being together. Vanity tapped him on the chest and said, "Well Mr. Bobbin, it looks like you still have some work to do. Standing here isn't going to change anything so what's your plan?"

Vanity told Dexter about Drexel plot without a plan idea. He was not surprised. He knew what his brother was capable of, just as he was. They were raised to protect the family at all cost. Dexter did not plan to hurt anyone but if someone got in the way, he would have no choice. He understood where Drexel was coming from but he did not like that he tried to use Vanity behind his back.

"Don't mention anything. Both of you are working towards the same goal. Maybe things will calm down on their own." Vanity tried to assure him.

"I wish I believed that. If Francine has tried to rat me out, then she intends to see this through. She's going for blood." Dexter explained.

"Be careful. I will be going back to San Francisco after the opening. I am not planning to stay here Dexter. I need you to know that."

"But...I thought that after today...."

"What, you thought that after we made love that things would back to where they were?"

"I mean...well...I was hoping."

"Dexter, as much as I love you and will always love you, I cannot uproot my life and move here. There is nothing for me here."

"So, I'm nothing? I thought..."

"Dexter, please stop. You are thinking too far ahead. Your first priority is dealing with your ex-wife. Not me."

"You are the priority. Dealing with Francine is so we can go on living our life together."

"Dexter, when did you decide that that was the reason? How about we have twins that she would love to get to because of you and me?"

"I know Vanity...I know...but I would like another chance."

Dexter grabbed Vanity and pulled her to him. He wanted to kiss her...he felt his nature rising and his heart beating faster. He was near her lips and he was leaning in for a kiss but they were interrupted.

"I'm sorry to interrupt but Dexter we need to talk." Drexel said.

"Excuse me." Dexter walked away adjusting his dick that had grown noticeably in his shorts.

He closed the door behind him. "Dexter, we need to handle this as soon as possible. Mansfield is working out the details of your new alias but we have to get Francine under control."

"I understand the urgency but what moves are you prepared to make at this point. We do not even know her angle. Why don't we call her?"

"I am past the talking point. If you don't handle this, then I will."

"Oh, you will? What are you going to do?" Dexter chuckled at the thought of his brother carrying out some master pre-meditated murder plan.

"I have already made the call. In less than 24 hours, it will be done. I did not think you had it in you." Drexel's eyes were dark and lifeless. Dexter became worried.

"Hey, Drexel, man...why are you so angry?"

"Why am I so angry!? It is because of you and your women. You are just like our father. Can have any woman in the world you want and you choose the crazy ones!"

"Hey, watch it. I was young and naïve back then. That is why I know Vanity is the one."

"The one? It doesn't sound like she agrees with you anymore." Drexel said.

"Were you eavesdropping on our conversation?" Dexter raised his eyebrow.

"Well, let's just say, you had better enjoy that pussy while it's here because she is going back to the US when this is all over."

"Are you jealous?"

"Of what? Don't flatter yourself."

"You know what...let's get this over with." Dexter said.

The brothers remained behind closed doors and devised what they thought would handle this situation with Francine and her family.

Vanity went up to her room and tried to settle in. Everything was just as she had left it. She laid across the bed to rest. Dexter had worn her out at the office and she needed a power nap. She did not care what they were planning to do with Francine; it did not have much to do with her at this point. All she knew was that they had better handle it soon or else everything would blow up and the entire family would be facing some jail time.

To Vanity, it seemed like only minutes that she had been asleep when she heard a tap on the door. It was Dexter.

"Come in."

"Sorry to wake you. I am going back to the US tomorrow."

"What? Why?" Vanity was a bit groggily but she was certain that she heard that Dexter was going to try to get back into the US.

"I have to. Drexel refuses to go." He said.

"What about Clayton?"

"What about him? I do not need him. I can handle this myself."

"And what exactly are you going to do."

"I have a lot of dirt on that family. I did not want to use it because of her children but she's pushed me to the limit."

"Why do you have to go there to handle it…and what type of dirt are you talking about?" Vanity asked now sitting up on the bed.

"Let's just say, they have a lot of skeletons in the closet that she doesn't know that I know about. If this comes out, it has to be anonymously."

"Then why can't I do that. You cannot go back to the US, Dexter. That's a death sentence."

"Are you willing to do this?" Dexter asked.

"If it is what it sounds like, yes. I am not going to be a murderer and knock her off but if I can get her ass thrown in jail for life, that I can do."

"Thank you Vanity. You do not know how much this means to us."

"Us?"

"I am talking about my family."

"Oh, okay. I do not want you getting any ideas about 'us'. What happened today was not an indication that we are back together. Let's be clear about that."

Dexter looked rejected but Vanity did not sympathize at all. She needed to get back to her life and there was no guarantee that Dexter would be part of it.

"Fine, Vanity. Please meet me down in the office so we can give you the details." Dexter walked away.

ten

"Welcome back to the United States." The gate agent stated and returned Vanity's passport. All of the arrangements had been made and all Vanity had to do was make a few calls, go see Francine and the McKnight's would handle the rest.

Leaving the airport and headed to her office, Vanity called her best friend, "Cole, it's me. Call me when you get this message." Vanity tried to reach Cole to tell her that she was back. She had not seen her or the kids since they returned from London weeks ago. The distance was a little odd but Vanity asked her to keep a low profile. She decided to call her daughter to check in.

"Hi mom." Christina answered.

"Hi honey. Are you at the office? I'm looking for Cole."

"Oh, Cole and Robert went on vacation to Disneyworld."

"In Florida?"

"Yea, they left two weeks ago when they came back from London. Why? What's up?"

"I need to update her on what's going on."

"What's going on? I can relay the message when she checks in."

"No, that's okay. I left her a message to call me back so I will wait to hear from her."

"Mom...will you stop treating me like a child. I can handle the information. I mean...nothing is a secret anymore."

"What do you mean? Nothing's a secret."

"Dexter being alive and all. I mean, there was a story on the news and the cops came by here to see if they could get information. They asked for you and Cole."

"Oh, my goodness. I did not know all of this was going on. Why didn't anyone call me?"

"Cole said not to. She knew you would worry and try to come back over here and fix things...like you always do and she wanted you to focus on your grand opening."

"Well thanks for trying to spare me. Now, I have to find out what is going on. Has everything else been okay?"

"Yes. We have some very big marketing campaigns coming up and I'll be launching those while Cole is out."

Vanity tried to remain calm and not cause alarm to Christina about this situation. Apparently, the story was a little more in depth than she thought. Vanity needed to ensure that she did not have any news crews posted up outside her doors.

"Okay, sweetie. When she calls, tell her I said to call me."

"Got it mother. They are due back tomorrow anyway."

Vanity tried to call her assistant but it went to voicemail so she called the receptionist.

"St. Christopher's how may I direct your call?" The receptionist asked.

"Hi Mona, its Van. Is Leslie in the office today?"

"Hi, Ms. Rodriquez. Yes, she is. She stepped out for lunch. She should be back any moment."

"Has there been any unusual visitors or activity around the office?"

"Well, yea. There was a guy who stopped by yesterday and said he was with the FBI but I could not tell by the way he was dressed. He asked for you but of course I told him you were out of the office."

"Did he leave his name or card?"

"Yes, he did. Do you want it?"

"Yes, please."

Vanity pulled over so she could take down the agent's information. She thought long and hard about what she would say when she called. The last thing she needed was the feds snooping around her front door. She needed to dispel any myth about what they heard and try to end their investigation.

"Agent Johnson, please."

"This is Johnson, how can I help you?"

"This is Vanity Rodriguez. I believe you came to my office yesterday."

"Oh, yes. I did. I need to speak to you about your former associate, Mr. Dexter McKnight."

"What about him? I mean he's dead."

"Ms. Rodriguez, are you available to meet me down at the café on Market Street?"

"Sure. We'll have to make it quick."

"Absolutely. I will not take up too much of your time. Can you meet in thirty minutes?" The agent asked.

"Yes. I will see you then."

Vanity did not plan on this detour but she had to move forward. She had a plane to catch to Vegas in the morning. On the way to the café, Vanity contemplated her answers to the agent's questions. She knew they would be very direct in wanting to know if she had seen or talked to him based on their tip. She also knew that because they did not ask her to come down to their office that she was not under arrest and that they were only fishing to see if she knew anything.

Her thoughts then went to Grant. The café on Market Street was their favorite place to go on Saturday afternoons when they did not have to work. Grant's coastal jobs always kept him busy on the weekends. Vanity felt a tug on her heart thinking about Grant. That is when she realized that she missed him. The man she missed so much was back in her life but could not forget about Grant and she did not know why. She tucked the question in the back of her mind. She had to focus on the task. She was a bit angry that she had to handle Dexter's dirty work. She had become the fixer. If it were not for Cassidy and Collin being at risk in all of this, she would have told Dexter and Drexel where they could shove all of this drama a long time ago.

When she pulled up to the café, she realized that she did not know what this agent looked like. She hoped he knew who he was looking for. When she got out of the car and headed into the café, a tall, slim built, Caucasian man stood up.

"Ms. Rodriguez." He said firmly extending his hand.

"Yes." Vanity shook his hand and looked him in the eye.

"This way." The agent directed Vanity to a corner booth inside the café.

"Thank you for meeting me on such short notice." Johnson said allowing Vanity to take a seat first inside the booth.

"It's no problem." Vanity said.

"Well, I will be brief and blunt. I hope that is okay." He said.

"I would appreciate that." Vanity said and looked down at her watch.

"We received an anonymous tip on the FBI line regarding the bombing you were involved in several years ago and the man you were dating at the time." He started.

Vanity listened intently and waited for an actual question.

"The tipster stated that Mr. McKnight had actually caused the bombing to fake his own death in order to flee the country. Do you know anything about that?"

"No." Vanity said.

"Do you know anything about Dexter McKnight faking his death?"

"No."

"Have you seen or heard from Dexter McKnight?"

"No."

Is there anything that you can tell me about your dealings with the McKnight family?"

There was the open-ended question that she had been expecting. There were details she felt were harmless to share while others, well, they were not because they would incriminate her and Dexter.

"I am the mother of his children, even though we have adopted them to my best friend. I have a relationship with his twin brother Drexel in London and as you already know, Dexter left his restaurant business to me – so yes, I still have dealings with Dexter's immediate family."

"Do you have any information that could help with this investigation?"

"What investigation?" Vanity was attempting to dispel the myth.

"The tipster provided additional information that we have been able to support. We just need to cover all bases."

"What bases, exactly?"

"You were his mistress and he left you a lot of money and from what I gathered, the wife was not too fond of that transaction."

"The wife?" Vanity almost sounded offended.

"Look, Ms. Rodriguez, I am not sure what you think you know about the McKnight's but if I were you, I would stand clear. There is a lot going on that you don't know about the late Dexter McKnight."

"Excuse me? You will not defame his name in that way. Now you look, I do not know what wild goose chase you're on but I am done here." Vanity scooted out of the booth and headed for the door.

"Wait…Ms. Rodriguez…" Agent Johnson yelled out after her.

Vanity turned abruptly to find him right on her heels, "Agent, unless you are taking me down to your office to speak to your commander, I am done here."

The agent stepped back and let her leave.

Vanity got into her car and sped off down the street. She was boiling with anger at what the agent accused Dexter of. Dexter had shown her nothing that would cause her to question him...well, except for the "pretending to be dead" part. At that point, she started to think about what the agent was talking about. What didn't she know? Why was Francine so persistent? She always had a hand to play. "It's time I get to the bottom of this." Vanity spoke aloud as she made her way out onto the 101 toward her beach house.

When she arrived, it was nearly sunset. Vanity intentionally rushed inside so she could make it out on the patio to watch the sun set for the night. She missed her view. She missed the simple life she was living only months ago when Grant was just her boyfriend. If they both made it home in time, he would get a beer and Vanity would get a glass of wine, go out on the patio, and watch the sunset. Even though Grant was raised near the beach all of his life, he never stopped appreciating it. It was the simple things that he liked that made Vanity stick around. It was not his job, his body or his sex. It was his innocence. Vanity felt alone in that moment – unlike she had in the past. Dexter wanted her back but she did not know what she wanted. The man she agreed to marry left her only months ago.

What is wrong with me? Vanity's thoughts were blaming her. *Karma cannot still be in effect.* Vanity tried to assure herself.

"Buzz....buzz" Vanity heard her phone vibrating on the kitchen counter. She snapped out of her thoughts and realized the sun had hypnotized her. She ran into the kitchen for the phone.

"Hello."

"Hi Van, it's me."

"Why are you calling me?"

"I wanted to know that you made it. I did not hear anything from you."

"Well, the plane did not fall out of the sky did it? Of course, I made it."

"Good." He ignored her sly remark, "I need to brief you on the latest."

"Look, De...Nigel...or whatever your name is. I am not in the mood to talk shop right now."

"Why not? That is why you are there, isn't it?"

"It is one of the reasons but I still have a business to run. Besides that, I am in the middle of enjoying a glass of wine."

"When are you going to Las Vegas?"

The doorbell rang.

"Hold on. Someone is at the door." Vanity said.

"Check before you open the door." Dexter said.

"Oh, boy...please stop it." Vanity said and peeped through the peephole anyway.

"Well, who is it?" He asked.

"It's Grant."

"Grant? What the hell is he doing there?"

Vanity had already opened the door.

"Hi Grant." Vanity was shocked to see him.

"Hi, Van. Are you busy?" He motioned to the phone.

"Oh...Hey, Nigel. I have to get back with you on that shoptalk. I will be in touch. My flight to Vegas is in the morning. I'll call you then."

"Vanity...what are you..."

Love on Fire

Vanity disconnected the call and properly greeted Grant and invited him in.

"What are you doing here?"

"I am taking a little time off. My mom went into the hospital and things were really touch and go for a while so I came home to see her."

"I'm sorry. How is she now?"

"Better. I will get a few other loose ends cleared up before I go back to the island."

"What are you doing out here?" Vanity asked sitting on the sofa.

"I just wanted to see you. I took a chance stopping by. I did not know if you were in town."

"Perfect timing. I just arrived today."

Grant pulled Vanity up from the sofa and embraced her tightly. She could feel the energy surging from him. He exhaled. He inhaled. He did not say a word. He just wanted to touch her and Vanity was melting within his grasp.

"I miss you." He said finally.

He pulled back from his embrace and looked into her eyes. "Tell me that I haven't lost you forever."

Vanity did not answer. She really did not know and this was not the time to make him feel good. She had to be honest with him.

"Grant, I miss you, too but I do not know where my heart is. I was just thinking about you sitting out there watching the sunset. You are a good man and I messed up."

"I should have never walked out." Grant confessed.

"You did what you had to do. I understand." Vanity really did understand but that did not change the feeling she felt when he walked out.

"Look, I shouldn't have come over. I should go." He turned to walk out.

"Stay. I mean, you came all this way." Vanity pleaded. She did not want to be alone.

"I guess I can stay for a while."

"Good. Would you like a beer or something? I am going back out on the patio."

"Sure." Grant went to the refrigerator and found that his half-drunken case of beer was still there. He twisted the top and took a long swig.

Vanity heard her phone buzzing from outside. She ignored it. It was Dexter probably wondering what she was doing.

"Your phone is ringing." Grant noticed it too.

"Yea, I know but I'm off duty. So, tell me about Curacao." Vanity asked leaning back in the chair and kicking her bare feet up on the railing.

Grant told Vanity about his job and the island that he lived on for the past couple of months. He described the beautiful water and the cultural people. "It's one of the most beautiful islands I've been to." He said.

"Maybe I'll travel there one day." Vanity said looking out at the Pacific Ocean like it was a busy mall full of interesting people.

"You'd love it." Grant said now kicking his feet up on the railing.

This was their spot. He sat in his chair and she sat in hers. At that moment, it felt like nothing had changed between them. Vanity felt herself dozing off, as she would typically do after a long day.

Vanity....a soft voice whispered in her ear. Vanity could not see his face but she knew his voice. It was sultry...it was masculine and it was confident. The voice came closer and moaned seductively this time. From behind, he wrapped his hand around her stomach and pulled her closer to him. With his other hand, he tilted her head to the side, grabbed a fist full of her curly locks and sucked on the back of her neck.

"Hmmmmm..." Vanity let out a moan. He kept his face from her sight. He lifted her dress and allowed the salt in the air to reach her wet spot. Dropping down on his knees, he spread her legs and hid himself under her dress, ready to pleasure her pussy. Vanity grabbed the railing and let out sensual sounds because no one could hear her. His tongue was more than her pleaser it was her master. It controlled her sound, her movement and the tingling sensation she felt with each suck and pull. "Ahhhh...." He knew when she was going to cum. These two were no strangers to each other. He knew her and she knew him. Their passion was not a façade. There was something about his energy; it was irreplaceable. He knew she was at her peak..."Oooooh...yeah...I'm coming...." The best position to squirt all over his face...and she did.

"Vanity...."

"Ahh!" Vanity jumped up in her seat.

"Are you okay?" He asked.

"Yea, I just dozed off." Vanity tried to straighten up.

"Is that all? You were moaning. Are you alright?"

"Oh, yea. I have been having weird dreams. It's nothing."

"Okay. Well, I am going to head out. I have to be back to relieve my sister. I agreed to do the night shift to keep an eye on mom."

"Oh…Okay." Vanity sounded disappointed.

"I will be in touch." Grant said taking his empty beer bottle inside.

"I'll walk you out."

Vanity walked Grant to the door and gave him a hug.

"It was good seeing you." He said exhaling from the hug.

"Yea. I appreciate you stopping by."

Vanity wanted Grant to stay but she could not bring herself to ask. It did not feel right and she knew it would be selfish and unfair of her to lead him on. Hell, she just had a wet dream about Dexter not even five minutes ago. Her emotions were all over the place. A good and decent man who lived a drama free life was walking out her door again. When the door closed, she leaned against it, slid to the floor and thought about when her life was simple…back in Las Vegas before Dexter. Her life was boring with her husband, Winston. Her routine was mundane. Her sex life was only alive because she made sure she got hers when she needed it. She had no worries.

V. Marie

Vanity was thinking back on these memories as she had done several times before when trying to make sense of her life...she had never accepted the truth. Her life was fine. Her marriage was boring but it was solid. She gave up a good life for someone who excited her sexually and even mentally but that turned into havoc and disrupted her life. When she thought she had her life back months ago, she did not. Dexter had been a constant thought in her mind. Even in his absence, he consumed her. "Damn him!" Vanity spewed aloud. That thought sent a surge of burning anger through her. There was only one way to fix this.

Vanity made her way to her room and packed a small bag for her Vegas trip the next morning. Going to bed early would get her mind off the madness and closer to wrapping things up. There was no room for error in the plan. Dexter was clear about that.

❤❤❤

Sometime after her release from prison, Francine relocated to Las Vegas. Vanity was already in California at the time so the thought of her never came up until recently. Vanity assumed that she had started a new life. Unfortunately, that was not the case and she was up to her old tricks again. Her family apparently was just bad news. There was no better way to put it. They were ruthless and Francine had it in her to be just as conniving without a care for the consequences. Trying to get Dexter caught by the US government after accepting a bribe was bold but she took that chance.

When Vanity arrived at her hotel, which was not on the strip for a change, she took some time to prepare for her meeting with Francine. She contacted Drexel to get an update before she set the plan in motion.

"Hi, Drexel."

"Vanity."

"I am at the hotel. How is everything?"

"Good to go. Just stick to what we discussed and you'll be in and out of there." Drexel said.

"Got it. How is everything else?"

"Everything else is fine. Just give me a call when your meeting is over."

"Okay."

Vanity disconnected the line and called a cab. The impromptu meeting was at The Paris hotel where Francine worked as her cover up job. After her release from prison, for being involved in Vanity's bombing accident, her employment options were quite limited. Vanity knew all about The Paris. Her firm did work for them over the years and although she had connections, she did not need to use them. The McKnight's were able to get everything they needed on their own.

When the cabby drove up to the hotel's revolving door, he told Vanity the fare and she paid him in cash. Inside the main foyer of the hotel Vanity checked her cellphone for the time. Francine would be ending her shift in 30 minutes.

Looking as if she had a long day at the office, Vanity found a seat at the bar in the casino. The bartender came over to the take her order, "Good evening ma'am, what can I..." the bartender stopped mid-sentence.

"Yes, I'll have a Honey Jack on the rocks." Vanity looked straight into Francine's eyes.

"What the hell are you doing here?" Francine said through her teeth.

"I'm sorry. Do I know you?" Vanity looked behind her as if Francine was talking to someone else.

"I'm talking to you. What the hell are you doing here?"

"I am sorry. You must have me mixed up with someone else. Can I have my drink please?" Vanity said pulling out cash from her purse.

There was mumbling of obscenities that Vanity could hear but she kept her cool. This was going quite well. She enjoyed getting under Francine's skin. If it were not for the fact that Francine tried to blow her up in the car, Vanity would have sympathized with the woman for all she had been through with Dexter but since she has resorted to extortion and trickery to get revenge, Vanity had no love for her and had to put a stop to the madness.

The drink made its way to the bar but Vanity had no intentions on drinking it. The likelihood that it had spit it in or some other unknown substance was quite high. Vanity let the drink sit on the bar for show. The call came in right on schedule.

"Hello, honey." Vanity said.

Francine only heard one side of the conversation as she pretended to look busy.

"Yes, baby. I know...yes, everything is fine. Stop worrying about me...oh, yes. I am taking care of that...Yes, baby. I love you, too. I will see you back at the hotel." Vanity hung up the phone. Francine could not help it.

"You think I give a damn about you and Dexter?"

"Oh, excuse me. What are you talking about? I do not know you, ma'am."

"Ma'am? Tssss!" Francine stormed away from the bar and off into the crowd of happy hour gamblers in the casino. Vanity checked her watch and she had about fifteen minutes before she would need to leave. Francine would be off work and surely be on her tail.

❤ ❤ ❤

Vanity hailed a taxi to head back to her hotel. "Downtown to the Fitzgerald, please." Vanity checked her watch.

"Yes, ma'am." The cab driver took off from the hotel and headed north on Las Vegas Boulevard. Once the car made a turn off the strip, Vanity looked out the back window to see if someone was behind them.

"Sir, the Fitzgerald is downtown. Where are you going?"

The driver did not answer. He only continued to drive and look up at his rearview mirror. Vanity looked back and saw a car riding closely behind them. Vanity discretely pulled out her cellphone and dialed.

She spoke aloud, "Sir, where are we going? This is not the way to the hotel." She waited for an answer but then she spoke louder for the caller on the other end of the phone, "Are you kidnapping me?"

"Ma'am please shut the fuck up. I am following orders. I don't want to hurt you...now be quiet!"

Vanity left the phone on so that wherever she was going she would at least be able to leave a GPS trace. Vanity knew the streets of Vegas and she was very much aware of where she was going on each turn. What she did not know was why they were going off course. This was not part of the plan.

Once they got on Route 15, Vanity started to worry. She looked at the car door to plan an escape but realized that there was no handle to open the door. The phone was still on but she was afraid to raise it to her face and draw attention.

They got off at the exit for the Motor Speedway and the driver pulled out his cellphone, "Boss, we are at the spot...uh yeah, I guess...okay got it."

Vanity could hear Dexter on the phone speaking and she immediately muffled the earpiece. She started to talk so he would listen, "Why are we at the Motor Speedway?"

"Ma'am I said do not talk. This will only take a minute." He responded.

"A minute? What the hell is going on?" Vanity became brave. This driver was obviously not in any position to do anything to her.

"Look, bitch, I said it'll be over in a minute."

Vanity did not see herself getting anywhere with this person. She had to let this play out. There was no move for her to play anyway. She felt trapped. All she could do was give clues.

"Is Francine involved in this?" She asked.

The driver ignored her.

"So, this is about Francine."

Love on Fire

The driver did not answer because he saw another car pull into the parking lot of the empty racetrack. It was a dark sedan with dark tinted windows. When the door opened, there she was. Francine. Two other men that Vanity did not recognize followed her.

"What is Francine and those men doing here?"

"You'll see." The driver said with a chuckle.

Francine approached and opened the door of the cab.

"Get out!" she yelled.

Vanity tried to hide the cellphone so that Francine did not notice it but it was too late.

"Give me that damn cellphone!" Francine snatched the phone, looked at the screen, and saw that it was on an active call.

"Hello? Hello?" She threw the phone down and one of the men crushed it with a mighty stomp.

"Who the fuck were you calling?" Francine asked.

Vanity did not speak.

"Nothing to say now? Finally, I get the blood I have been waiting for. You ruined my family and took my money."

Vanity still did not speak.

"You had me thrown in jail and my children hate me. You ruined my fucking life with your affair with my husband!"

Vanity looked Francine in the eye, "You ruined your own life with your greed. I never asked for this and I sure as hell never asked for his money. It has caused me more problems than I can count and he is not your husband anymore."

"Well, it doesn't matter now. I am over him and you. Dexter thinks that I do not know he sent you. I am not a foolish woman. He should know better."

Vanity changed her posture and matched Francine. This pissing match was going nowhere and whatever was going to go down was going down whether Dexter sent the cavalry or not. She had to stand up to Francine or back down.

"Francine, I do not know what you think your end game is here but money has a paper trail and you're already being watched for your last blackmail attempt." Vanity spat.

"I'm not out for money with you. I'm out for blood." Francine looked starkly in Vanity's eyes.

"Poncho, take this broad to the car. We're going for a ride," the man said.

Poncho was Francine's youngest cousin. He did the grunt work and yanking Vanity by the arm, he did that with pleasure.

"Get in!" He forced Vanity head first into the backseat.

Vanity sat quietly in the backseat still observing the surroundings. They had literally drove her out to a vacant parking lot to do who knows what. She became angry with Dexter and Drexel for putting her in this situation. Then she thought about Christina and the twins. The children did not deserve to be involved in any of this. For what? Love? This is not love. This is not how love works. The thought of love being the reason infuriated Vanity even more. The life she started with Grant was possibly on its way to marital bliss. The one man who she opened up to after Dexter. Vanity refused to cry. This was a bad time for that but her heart was hurt for all of the lives she had affected with her lust and relationship with Dexter, one that put her life in jeopardy once again.

"Dear God..." Vanity started a silent prayer and had it interrupted by the driver's side door opening.

"Buckle up." The sound of a familiar voice.

"Clayton?" Vanity gasped.

Francine opened the car door to get into the passenger's seat. "I see you two have been reacquainted." Francine chuckled.

"How could you?" Vanity managed to say.

"Bitch, please. Dexter isn't the only one with loyal friends. From what I heard, Clayton was available for hire...so here we are."

"That's what this is about, money? What is it with *you* people?"

"*You* people?" Francine twisted her neck around to ensure Vanity saw her disgust with the question.

"Yes, you people. Money is not going to solve all of your damn problems and if you think that killing me will give you the pleasure of spending more money – then you are mistaken. This is not a Hollywood movie. You cannot kill people and get away with it."

"You haven't seen my new hire's work before have you?" Francine patted Clayton on the shoulder.

Love on Fire

Clayton wore his firm steel persona. Nothing Vanity said moved him nor did he respond. There was always something eerie about Clayton but Vanity trusted him because of Dexter but now she started to think about all of the times she was alone with him and she thought he was protecting her. Was he loyal then? Vanity did not know. Everything was spiraling out of control.

"Where are we going?" Vanity insisted.

"Put the blindfold on her." Clayton directed.

Francine pulled out a gun and pointed it at Vanity. "Put this on – and don't even think about removing it unless I tell you to."

Vanity put the blindfold on as she looked down the barrow of the 9 mm. The rest of the ride, Vanity tried to recall the turns and distances but it became too winding and she lost track severely. All she had to hold onto was her purse.

The drive was not as long as she thought and when the car started to slow down, she heard the crackling sound of rocks beneath the tires. When the door opened, Vanity could smell the horse manure in the air. Wherever they were, it was definitely away from the city. The only sounds she heard were from the animals.

V. Marie

Vanity felt a pull on her arm, "Get out the car."

It was Clayton. Vanity yanked her arm away from him and spat in his direction. He raised his hand to slap her but Francine grabbed his arm.

"Not yet. Calm down. Here wipe your face." Francine pulled out a crumpled up bar napkin from her pocket.

"That bitch." Clayton mumbled.

Poncho came over at Francine's beckoning and took hold of Vanity's arm. Francine tossed a rope over to her cousin to tie up her arms, "If you spit on me, Francine will not be able to save ya." He said.

Vanity recognized the voice as the man who put her in the car. She walked with them for several hundred feet. The stench of horseshit worsened the more they walked. Vanity did not try to fight; she couldn't. She put her thoughts in a place that only God could hear. The rest of her life would be dictated by these next few moments or possible the last few moments.

Vanity could hear Clayton and Francine talking in a low tone. They did not seem to be in agreement with something. Poncho was tailing so far behind that Vanity could not quite make out what it was about. Dexter would be so disappointed. All of this time she thought he had a loyal friend and partner; turns out, he was sleeping with the enemy all along. Everything he ever said to Vanity was invalidated – he is one of them and as far as Vanity was concerned, he always was.

"Bring her in here." Francine said.

"What are we...?" Vanity started to ask.

"You don't get to ask questions here." Clayton butt in.

"Francine," Vanity dismissed Clayton's comment, "What are we doing here?"

"The fact that you're still blindfolded means that there is something about to happen to you that – you may not want to see coming." Francine smirked.

The sound of a helicopter was churning overhead. "Boss! There is a helicopter touching down out here! Are you expecting somebody?"

"Hell, no! Who the hell is it?" Francine pushed Vanity into a stall and closed the door.

"I don't know. I've never seen this guy before." Poncho called out over the loud chopper.

"Let me go check it out." Clayton said leaving Francine to guard the door with Vanity.

"Hurry up. I want to get this over with." Francine said.

By the time Clayton had reached the door of the barn and turned the corner, Poncho hit the ground. "Gun!"

Clayton dove under the barrel of hay to take cover. Francine opened the stall door and pushed Vanity down on the haystack. "Say one word and I will shot your ass." She poked the 9 mm in Vanity ribcage.

A few more shots fired and then several more. Vanity did not know who or what was going on but she hoped it was the Calvary. She did not know how much more of this she could take.

The sound of doors opening and closing became louder and louder. When the door flung open to where Vanity and Francine sat on the haystack, shots went off. Vanity, yelped because she could not see anything and she could not move. Francine let go of Vanity's arm and she heard a thump on the hay.

"Are you OK?"

Vanity knew his voice even with the blindfold on "Grant? What are you doing here? How did you..."

Grant pulled off the blindfold and untied her arms. "Do not question anything at this moment. I have to get you out of here." He scooped up Vanity and trotted out to the chopper.

Grant helped Vanity onto the chopper, and then gave the chopper the signal to lift off.

"Wait!" Vanity tried to say when she realized he was not going with her but it was too late, the chopper roared and started in an upward motion.

"Fasten your seatbelt ma'am." The pilot said.

Vanity complied and as she looked down at the ground. A tow truck and two vans pulled into the yard. Whatever just happened, they must be the clean-up crew. Before she knew it, they were back over the bright lights of Las Vegas Boulevard.

Vanity never thought she would be so happy to see Sin City. That half of a prayer to God must have made it all the way. Whatever was supposed to happen by the hand of Francine did not happen; now what was left of her and her goons – Vanity preferred not to know – at least not right now. Dexter was most likely involved but Grant...the thought made her question who he was. Had he been working with Dexter all along? At that moment, Vanity figured it did not matter. He saved her life.

eleven

As the adrenaline calmed down and Vanity felt safe in the sky flying across the city, she closed her eyes. The sun was not quite set but feeling it bleed through her closed eyelids made her remember her home that once faced west and gave her a dose of sunset every night. She missed that and the simple things that life used to offer. Vanity wanted *that* life. The life that was simple but passionately hot just like the sun.

When the chopper landed on top of the Palm hotel just off the strip, Vanity opened her eyes. An escort was waiting to assist her with disembarking.

"This way ma'am."

"Thank you."

Just inside at the Penthouse level, the escort escorted Vanity to her room.

"What am I doing here?" Vanity felt as if she had asked that question all night and no one would answer her but she took another stab at this new guy. He looked nice and she was certain this was not a gift from the Francine goon squad.

"Ma'am, the room is prepared for you to rest. Your travel itinerary is on the night stand." The escort pulled the door closed and left Vanity alone in the oversized room.

Over on the nightstand, Vanity saw an envelope with her name on it. It was a ticket to London leaving McCarran International the next day.

"Dexter, what are you doing to my life? I am not ready for this trip so soon." Vanity spoke aloud as she read the plane ticket.

Vanity could only shake her head. She did not have a way to call him and from the looks of it, he had his mind made up.

Hot water was the only thing Vanity could think of to calm her down. Getting angry would not help because he did save her life or was it Grant, she thought. Either way, going back to London was his plan to get her away from Grant. She was sure of that.

In the bathroom, Vanity saw the bag she had left at the Fitzgerald and another small suitcase with clothing, makeup and other essentials and a cell phone. She turned on the cellphone and called Dexter.

"Are you okay?" He said immediately.

"Yes. What happened?"

"Honey, you did great. Everything is done."

"What? What do you mean? I was two seconds away from being shot by that crazy woman!"

"She played right into our hand."

"Our hand? Who are you talking about? Clayton was with Francine. He is a traitor!"

"Calm down. He is not a traitor. Clayton is the only loyal friend I have. He would never cross me."

"It did not look like it. They seemed awfully close."

"As I said, she played right into our hand."

"How did Grant get involved? I mean, what is going on, Dexter. I'm confused."

"Clayton needed to use someone that Francine would not know. He knew Grant would do whatever to keep you safe and he jumped on it."

"You used him? And me? You set this whole thing up. You bastard!" Vanity yelled.

"Vanity, please calm down. You did your part, just as I asked. You did great. If you knew the whole plan, it would not have worked. Please believe me."

"Why did you use Grant?"

"He was the only person I could trust to get you out of there."

"But he loves me Dexter. Now you expect me to leave for London tomorrow as if today did not happen. I thought I was about to die at the hands of your fuckin' ex-wife."

Vanity was furious and the longer she stayed on the phone the angrier she got. Dexter was not able to fix this with words and an explanation. Vanity was in the dark – completely.

"Dexter, I think I need to take some time to figure this out. I cannot return to London tomorrow. I need to spend some time with my family and redirect some things. I am emotionally exhausted."

"So what are you saying? What about the restaurant?"

"Oh, don't worry about the restaurant. It will launch and I will make sure it is a success. I am talking about you. You have made it your business to control my life and it is time for me to take over. You are alive and well. I could not be happier to know that your presence is still among us, but as for you and I...yea, I need a mental break. Good bye, Dexter." Vanity hung up before Dexter could even respond. She powered off the cellphone and started her bath.

Vanity laid her head back on the rest in the oversized Jacuzzi. She closed her eyes and she exhaled. Francine was finally out of her life. Dexter was put on the back burner. She felt free – at least for now.

❤❤❤

"Cole, call me at this number 555-0308 Room 5579, I am in town on business and I want to see you." Vanity wanted to catch up and see how things have been going since she had been gone.

When she woke up that morning and opened the curtains, the sun burst in like it was truly a new sun. The coffee she ordered from room service was no match to the satisfaction Vanity received from being able to see the natural element of the sunbeam against her face.

Love on Fire

The Palm overlooked the best parts of the strip and because of that; Vanity could see the all of the hotels under construction. VanCole was probably very busy with all of the new business coming to the city. It put a smile on her face to know that the stock she earned from VanCole were going into a trust for Christina and the twins.

Vanity was startled from her thoughts when the hotel phone rang. "Hello."

"Hey sis, what are you doing here?" Cole asked.

"I had a little business to take care of but I'll be here a few more days. I want to come by the office and check on things." Vanity said.

"I'd love for you to come by. I want to show you pictures from the vacation to Disneyworld." Cole said.

"Can't wait. What time?" Vanity asked.

"I'm headed there now but you can come by anytime. I have a few meetings but you can always sit in. I'd love to have you for a few days." Cole pleaded.

"Hey, I'm not here to do work for you!" Vanity laughed.

"You still owe me!" Cole reminded Vanity.

"You don't have to remind me." Vanity said.

"So that means you'll sit in on this presentation for the Blu Hotel."

"I've heard of the Blu Hotel. I would love to see the plan you designed for them. I will see you in an hour or so."

"Have you talked to the McKnight's lately?" Cole slipped in that question before Vanity could hang up.

"Uh, yea but I'll tell you about that later. Let me get dressed so I can get out of here."

Vanity went to the suitcase that was in the bathroom to see what Dexter packed. She pulled out a wrinkle free blue and white fitted dress and a complimenting pair of open toe heels. "Perfect," she said.

When the elevator finally made it to the lobby level, Vanity stepped out and strutted across the marble floor toward the exit while turning heads of the men on her left and right.

Moments like this reminded her that she had worked hard to get the life she had. Dexter did not make her and he sure as hell would not break her. Vanity had arranged for car service for the remainder of her time in Vegas. She had had enough of taxis. It would be a long while, if ever; that she would get into another cab.

Vanity spent the day with Cole and Christina going over the changes that the executives of the Blu Hotel wanted. It turned out to be a nice get away from the restaurant planning that she had been doing lately. It reminded her of why she went into business for herself in the first place. The leader in her could not sit back and just watch; she had to be involved.

"Chris, at the next presentation, why don't you give these young executives the new changes."

"Why? This is Cole's deal."

"Yea, Christina. I agree with your mother. These guys were a lot younger than I thought and I saw one of them eyeing you." Cole agreed.

"Oh, no. You want me to flirt with these guys!" Christina looked wide-eyed.

"Just enough to get the point across." Vanity smiled and looked over at Cole.

"Exactly. We do it all the time. How do you think we ended up marketing for half of the hotels and businesses on the strip? It was not from looking like a couple of old maids!" Cole reached across the table and gave Vanity a high five.

Vanity and Cole laughed for a few seconds and it trailed off into an awkward silence.

"We're getting old and we need some youthful sexiness around here." Vanity said.

"That's right." Cole said.

"And you need a makeover, my dear. You look like you are still in college. Spend some of this money you're making and upgrade your wardrobe."

"But mom...you know I don't get into all of the name brands."

"You don't have to. I will do it for you. You do not have to know the names. You just wear them and the names will speak for you." Another high five from Cole in agreement with Vanity.

"Fine." Christina finally agreed.

"The follow up meeting is tomorrow. We need to get started." Vanity said.

"You two go ahead and I will update the presentation." Cole said.

"Then off we go." Vanity said to Christina who knew that meant they were going to the mall.

"Sure." Christina said.

"You're so like your father." Vanity chuckled.

Vanity knew it would be torture for Christina to spend time and even money in the mall buying a few new outfits but it was time. Their business was all about presentation and it was the fancy $5,000 ensembles that made Vanity feel attractive and confident across the table from multi-billionaires.

❤❤❤

After shopping Vanity sent Christina to the salon for the final touches. It took a few extra pushes to get her to agree to a new cut and style but it worked out. By the time, Vanity returned to the hotel, she was exhausted.

She ran a hot bath and turned on the stereo to play Enya from her phone app. When she headed toward the bathroom, she heard a tap on the door. "Ugghh," she groaned. Vanity put the plush white robe on and went to the door. She peeped through hole and saw Grant.

"What are you doing here?" Vanity said through the crack she made in the door.

"I had to see you and make sure you were OK." He said.

"Why are you here? I do not want anything to do with none of this anymore. I don't know who you are or who you're working for either." Vanity said as she prepared to close the door.

"Wait. Don't do this Vanity." Grant put his hand on the door to keep it from closing."

"Do what?" She asked.

"Accuse me of being like them. I was only there because he told me you were in danger. That is all I knew. They told me if I did not go and help them she would hurt you again."

"What do you mean?" Vanity opened the door wider, revealing her white robe.

"I cannot give you all of the details but I know who that woman was and what she did to you. Vanity, I love you from my heart and I only want you to be safe."

"Grant, what did Dexter ask you to do?"

"Dexter?" Grant repeated.

"Yes, Dexter."

"What does he have to do with this?"

"Oh, my goodness. What has he done?"

"Vanity, what? Why are you asking me about your dead ex-lover?"

"Dexter is the reason why I was there. Who came for you? How did you know I was there?"

"Clayton. The man who kept showing up at your place. He told me the story and what happened and he said they needed a face that no one would recognize but that you would." Grant explained. "They said you were kidnapped." He finished.

"Those bastards."

Vanity opened the door and Grant came into the room. She started to see the cloud that was starting to go away quickly returning. The dark cloud of karma.

"Vanity, you have to tell me what is going on. Why is Dexter involved in this? He is dead isn't he?"

Vanity decided that she owed it to Grant to tell him the whole truth. Even the fact that Dexter was alive. He became furious and tried to leave the room in a rage but Vanity blocked him.

"Grant I can't let you leave like this. Remember, this does not only affect me. My twins and my friends are associated with this. We have to find a way to put this behind us." Vanity said facing Grant with her back against the door.

Grant approached Vanity and cupped her chin in the palm of his hand. He lifted her face and placed a sensual kiss on her lips. He stayed there for more than a few seconds, nearly stopped breathing as if he was dying in that moment just to kiss her. Vanity did not move.

Grant tugged on the tie of the robe and Vanity finally snapped back. "Wait…"

"Don't do this, Van…don't turn me away. Not now." Grant pleaded.

"I can't do this Grant. I am not sure what I am feeling right now." Vanity said.

Grant let out a sigh as if he knew what that meant. "Is this about him?"

"No. This is about me. I have to decide what I am going to do and I cannot do that if we're in bed together." Vanity explained.

"Then, let me leave. I see you are doing fine. I'm heading back to LA tomorrow and then back to the coast in a couple days."

"Oh. I did not know you were going back to the island. I thought you were taking care of your mother." Vanity said.

"Yea, well, I have to make a living. My sister will be okay. Besides, I came into a little money. I'll be able to come visit more often." Grant said.

Grant gave Vanity a kiss on the cheek and she stepped aside so he could leave the room. He left Vanity with thoughts about this whole situation.

"Just a moment." Vanity made her way to the door. When she opened it, Dexter stood there in dark shades and a black three-piece suit holding a bouquet of what looked like a hundred roses. He hid well behind his disguise but Vanity could recognize him.

"Get in here!" Vanity said pulling him inside and looking out the door and down the hall to make sure no one was out there.

"Calm down. There is no one there. I booked all of the rooms on this floor so we're alone." Dexter said.

"There is no limit with you is there?" Vanity said with a hint of attitude.

"I came to see you. You are not taking my calls. These are for you." He held out the roses.

"Thank you but I am not falling for that."

"Falling for what? I only came to make peace."

"Peace? You killed Francine and you hired Grant to do it."

"Hold on a minute. Who told you that?"

"Don't worry about who told me. You used Grant and me. I am done with this. All of it."

"Vanity, you don't know what you're talking about." Dexter insisted.

"Well enlighten me then."

Vanity went to the sofa in the suite and took a seat. She crossed her legs and sat back with her arms folded. Dexter came over and sat in front of her on the coffee table.

Dexter told Vanity the play-by-play sequence of events. He admitted to keeping her in the dark only to protect her in the event the plan fell through. He did not want to risk any mistakes.

"So, are you and Clayton still working together?"

"Yes. Clayton will always be loyal to me. He knows that our linkage is only broken by death."

"Death? What the hell does that mean?"

"It means that we have a brotherhood that cannot be broken. There isn't any amount of money or pussy that could come between Clayton and me. Francine doesn't know that and she fell for his ploy to get close to me."

"What about Grant? Why him?"

"Vanity, we had to use someone she did not know but who you would trust. I did not have a choice. Why does he matter to you anyway?" Dexter seemed jealous.

"You used him and you know he loves me. That was wrong and it confuses things."

"Confuses things? Why?"

"Because..." Vanity started to explain but Dexter did not let her finish.

He scooted the coffee table back just enough to make room in front of Vanity on the sofa. He got down on his knees and laid his head in her lap. "Please, don't say anything more."

"But..."

"Please."

Dexter reached in his jacket pocket and pulled out a black satin box. He sat it on the on the sofa cushion.

"Dexter, what is this?" Vanity pretended not to know.

"Now that I can, I want to make you my wife." Dexter admitted.

"Will you marry me?" Dexter opened the box and Vanity gasped at the ring that matched the yellow canary diamond earrings she already received.

"Dexter..." Vanity's voice was shaky.

"You are the love of my life. I cannot imagine you living with anyone else...making love to anyone else."

Vanity was silent. The ring was beautiful but she could not respond. Her heart was fluttering and her stomach was in knots. She looked into his eyes and said, "Yes."

"Beep! Beep! Beep!" The alarm sounded.

Vanity jumped up and realized that she had another dream. "Got dammit!"

It was clear. Dexter still had her heart no matter how upset she was with him. He stole her heart from the first time he made love to her and he was not giving it back. Vanity was not even sure she wanted him to. She quickly recalled the dream and thought about the proposal. Is that what Dexter's goal was? Did he take care of Francine so he could finally live his life with Vanity? Is that what the whole plot was about? The unanswered questions only created more questions and Vanity knew the only way to know was to face Dexter.

twelve

"Welcome home." The butler said as he escorted Vanity from the limousine.

"Thank you."

"I will carry your bags to your room. Lunch is served in the dining hall, ma'am. The McKnight's are awaiting your arrival."

"Thank you."

Vanity made her way through the estate to the dining hall. The hallway reminded her of walking through a museum. The paintings and artwork was expensive and probably one of a kinds. She had grown to like a few of the artists that were hanging around in different parts of the house.

"Gentlemen." Vanity said walking into the room.

"Vanity." Dexter stood and came over to assist her with the chair. He kissed her on the cheek before returning to his seat.

"Welcome back." Drexel said once Dexter was back to his seat.

"Look, I am not here for niceties. I want to know what happened back in Vegas and I don't want either of you to bullshit me."

"Vanity, please no profanity." Drexel said.

"What did I just say?" She looked at Dexter instead with an evil eye.

"Drexel, would you please excuse us?" Dexter asked.

"No. He needs to stay. I need both of you to tell me how you handled this situation while using me and Grant to do it." Vanity insisted.

"Fine, but before you get upset about Grant, you know how I feel about him. This mission was about us – our family. You are my family regardless of whether or not you've accepted that." Dexter said.

"I get all of that but tell me what does that have to do with this mission you sent me on and then it turned into something out of a damn movie." Vanity said.

"I know it looks like that but trust me. We did it so that Francine would believe it. Clayton had it all under control."

"What did you do to her?"

"I can't tell you."

"Why not?"

"It's for your own good that you don't know."

"Is she dead?"

"Vanity, please. I cannot tell you that." Dexter's response made Vanity uncomfortable.

"Vanity," Drexel interjected. "It's for the best. We are only thinking about you by keeping it from you. Besides, we want you to get focused on the restaurant again and the family business."

"It's kind of hard to do that when so much violence is going on around me." Vanity said.

"That's all behind us." Dexter said.

"Well, I wish I could trust that but I don't know what to think anymore."

"The grand opening is all you need to focus on."

"Yea, I will. I do have one more question."

"Do you still have Clayton on payroll?"

"I just use him when I need to."

"Well, I know he is the reason Grant got involved and I want you to stop contacting him. Do you understand?"

"Yes. I should not need to contact him ever again. Can I ask the same of you?" Dexter asked.

"I am free to contact whomever I like. Dexter, you and I are not in a relationship, remember." Vanity said matter of fact.

Drexel cleared his throat and was about to leave the dining table but Vanity beat him to it.

"Wait, where are you going?"

"Out. I need some air."

❤❤❤

Vanity had a car take her to the city to get away from them. Putting space between herself and the McKnight's was the only thing she could think of. The downtown London scene was lively. Vanity found a club on Charterhouse Street that had music nearly spilling out into the streets. Vanity was drawn to it. Music. It was something she once loved but all of the drama around her consumed her life. She went inside and lost herself in the music.

"Can I get you a drink?" The server asked as Vanity found her way into one of the many rooms in the club.

"I will have a martini." Vanity said.

The music was moving her body and she did not even realize it. By the time the drink arrived, she was already dancing. She nearly spilled the martini trying to sip it from the wide rim.

After a couple drinks, Vanity lost herself in the club. The music was techno and that meant, keep moving. A few men danced with her but she was into her own world. The last thing she wanted was too much attention from men.

After leaving the bathroom, Vanity checked her watch and realized she had been in the club for more than four hours. The dark rooms and music nearly hypnotized her. On the way toward the exit, Vanity ran into a man turning the corner.

"There you are! Vanity, what are you doing?"

"What are you doing? Are you following me?" Vanity said.

"You've been gone too long and I was worried."

"How did you know I was here?"

"The driver told me you said not to tell but he knew better. Are you okay?"

"Yes." Vanity straighten her posture trying to cover up her drunkenness.

"Come on, let's get you home." Dexter tried to grab onto Vanity's arm but she jerked it away.

"Let go of me. I am not going anywhere!"

"Van, please. It's time to go." Dexter grabbed her arm more firmly.

"Ouch, you're hurting my arm."

"You're drunk and I am taking you home."

"I don't want to go anywhere with you. You're a liar." Vanity said trying to pull her arm from his grasp but could not.

"We'll talk when we get to the car." Dexter steered Vanity out of the club.

Vanity did not try to resist Dexter anymore. She went more willingly to the car. When she stepped outside her ears were ringing from the music in the club. The air was clear and brisk. The light wind blew her hair over her face. Dexter noticed and pulled it back for her. At the curb, Dexter motioned for the Lincoln to pick them up.

"Watch your step." Dexter said helping Vanity in the car.

Vanity flopped in the seat and moved as close to the door as she could. Dexter sat opposite her, giving Vanity the space she wanted.

"Vanity, what is wrong with you?"

Silence.

"Why are you acting so distant and strange? I thought you would happy that we can be together."

Still silence.

Dexter waited for a response but instead he heard sniffling. He moved closer to her and pulled back her hair to reveal her face filled with streaks of tears.

"Talk to me."

"I am scared to love you again." Vanity said with her face toward the window.

"Why?"

"I don't trust you."

Dexter was silent. He sat back on the seat and exhaled. He did not know how to respond to that. Dexter looked up toward the driver and pressed the button to close the partition.

"I understand how you feel but I want another chance. I owe you everything for helping me get my life back."

Vanity turned her head to look at him, "What are you talking about?"

"Vanity, look...I have been dodging Francine more than anyone. I could not go on with my life with her hunting me down and chasing my money."

"Tell me what you did to her."

"Vanity, I cannot. Trust me...you do not want to know. "

"How do I start over and you can't tell me this?"

"If I tell you and someone questioned you, then you would have to tell them and I don't want you in that position."

"Is she dead?"

"She will not bother us again."

"Is she dead?" Vanity insisted.

"When we get back to the house we can finish talking about this."

"No! Tell me!"

"Vanity, don't push."

"Tell me!"

"I can't! It is best that you do not know any details. Now leave it alone. We did what we had to do."

"We? You mean Grant?" Vanity corrected.

"No. That is not what I said. I did not assign him to that task."

"Task?" Vanity chuckled.

"You know what I mean. I only had him there for interference and clean up."

"That's all he did?"

"Yes. Why? What is it with you and this Grant? Do you still want to be with him?"

"I don't know."

"What do you mean you don't know?"

"Like I said, I don't know."

"I did not do all of this for me. It was for us."

"Dexter, please stop saying that."

"It is the truth." Dexter turned Vanity's face toward him, "I did this for us. We need a do-over."

Vanity's eyes filled with more tears. For the past five years, she had been fighting this feeling of emptiness from losing her lover. She tried to fill it with what was in front of her but that did not work at first but it was starting to. Now, the day finally arrived and it was not a dream. Dexter is alive and practically begging for another chance.

Not paying much attention to the road they were traveling, Vanity noticed they pulled into the hotel at Dunston Hall. The hotel she stayed at when she first came to London. When the car pulled into the circular driveway, Dexter tapped on the partition window.

"Yes, Mr. McKnight?" the driver asked.

"Thank you. Give Drexel the message as I told you."

"Yes, sir."

Since Dexter did not get his answer yet, he helped Vanity out of the car.

"Vanity, let's go inside."

Vanity obliged and followed Dexter through the lobby.

Inside the room, Vanity noticed that it was already prepared for them. The ambience was set for a honeymoon.   Roses, wine and soft music were among the things she noticed at a glance.

"What's all this?"

"Shhh." Dexter put his finger over his lips.

Dexter walked passed the dining room and to the bedroom. Vanity was not surprised that he had thought of everything. A nightie and slippers were waiting for her. The housekeeper filled the Jacuzzi and Vanity could smell the lavender in the room. The alcohol that she had drank earlier had started to wear off. Everything around her was so peaceful and clear. Vanity pulled the dress over her head and revealed her body. Dexter only watched. She removed her bra and bikini panties and left everything in a pile on the floor. She went to the step to the Jacuzzi and turned back to look at Dexter. He rushed to her aid to assist her.

Vanity let out a relaxing sigh. "This is so relaxing. My feet hurt from so much dancing."

"Just relax. I'll get you some water."

"Thank you."

The soft music played in the background and Vanity laid her head back and closed her eyes. What is Dexter doing she thought? He was trying to seduce her. Vanity was too weak to fuss, tell him off or even refuse his gestures.

"Here is some water. Take a drink to re-hydrate." Dexter handed the glass to Vanity.

"Thank you." She sipped the water.

Love on Fire

Vanity closed her eyes again. Dexter made a small splash when he stepped into the tub. Vanity opened he eyes slightly and closed them again.

Dexter kissed her ear...her cheek and neck. "Hmmmm," Vanity let out a moan. Dexter kissed them again...her ear...her cheek and neck. Vanity grabbed his head as it moved down to her shoulder, the lowest he could go above water. He took her breast in his hand and softly pinched her nipples. Vanity could feel her vagina warming from his touch. Dexter took the sponge soaked up the soapy water and pressed it against her chest so the stream could run down her body making a splash into the water. After a few sponge downs, Dexter sat up on the ledge of the Jacuzzi. Vanity's body was at its ultimate point of relaxation. "Come to me." Dexter said.

Vanity stood and the water fell from her body into the Jacuzzi. Dexter guided her to him. Her breast in the right position to be kissed by his juicy lips. Vanity grabbed his head as he sucked on her ripe nipples. A moan escaped her.

He lifted her onto his lap where his dick fit perfectly into her pussy. "Hmmmm," she moaned.

His slow grind was amazing and satisfying. His ability to do the lifting gave Vanity a chance to feel the exchange of energy as the head of his dick massaged her g-spot. The electricity got stronger and stronger. Her head fell back and her arms dangled over his shoulders. He lifted her slowly and steady as if he was bench-pressing. His stamina was back without a doubt. His posture was perfect as he lifted his prize up and down on his hard dick. Vanity opened her eyes and looked into his and the intense stare brought them closer and closer. Vanity could feel her orgasm approaching and Dexter could feel it too. He was ready for it. "Ahhhhh...shit!" Vanity threw her head back contributing to the final grinds to fulfill her orgasm. Dexter stood up holding Vanity in place. He went to the steps and carried her out of the tub and into the bedroom.

He laid Vanity on the bed and her body still wet from the tub, Dexter pulled the comforter over her to keep her warm. Vanity was expecting to feel his tongue on her clit but instead he got into the bed next to Vanity and spooned her. She adjusted to lay her head on her bicep and he wrapped his arm under her and secured her tightly. His dick was still erect but he did not enter her. Dexter held her. He smelled her hair and exhaled.

"This is what I love. You here in my arms. Your ass on my dick. Your breast in my hands," Dexter gently squeezed her breast.

Vanity did not respond. She understood what was happening. Dexter was making love to her with intimacy and she needed it. Having sex with Dexter, even from the beginning was so passionate that she wanted it every chance she got. It was intimacy that they could not have – and have it freely. He chose tonight to do that. Vanity accepted him. He pulled her closer and before she knew it, Dexter was sound asleep. The sweet sound of his soft slumber tickled her ears. A smile turned up on her face as Vanity, also closed her eyes and let the moment settle in.

The stark ringing of the hotel phone broke their sleep. Dexter rolled over and answered, "Hello." He said groggily. "Yes…yea, okay, I got it man, damn." Dexter hung up the phone irritated.

"Everything alright?"

"My brother sweating me about some business after I told him I was checking out for a couple days."

"Couple days?"

"Yes. A couple days. We aren't going anywhere today," Dexter snuggled back up on Vanity's ass. This time, his dick was trying to gain a little access.

"Is that so?" Vanity lifted her leg giving Dexter a little assistance.

When he landed into the right spot, Dexter moaned and pulled Vanity closer. He tight slow grind from the back was hitting the top of her g-spot. He knew this nut would not take long. Vanity was electrifying and he could feel it. He rolled her onto her stomach and laid it into her from the back. Dexter laid low so he could stay slow and deep. Vanity lifted her ass slightly to meet him. When the feeling became too intense, Vanity started to shiver and Dexter knew he had her ripe and ready.

"Ahhhhh," Vanity let out a sensual scream to express her pleasure and satisfaction. Dexter was seconds behind her with his grunt and monstrous roar, "Uughhh!"

Love on Fire

He fell on the side of Vanity and looked at how beautiful she was. "What?" Vanity asked looking at Dexter looking at her.

"You are everything to me. I have only you. Do you understand that?" Dexter said.

Vanity did not respond at first. She thought about what he was saying. His mother was thousands of miles away. The kids he raised were not his. The kids that are his, he could not raise them because of the adoption. "You have Drexel." Vanity offered.

"That's not what I mean." Dexter disagreed with her.

"Then what do you mean?"

"You know what I want Vanity."

"What Dexter? What do you want?"

"I want you in my life now and forever. I do not want you to go back. I want to spend every night with you. I want to wake up every morning to you."

"Awww," Vanity rubbed the stubble on Dexter's beard and kissed his lips. "I'm hungry."

"Hungry? I'm pouring my heart out to you and you're hungry?" Dexter tickled Vanity under her arm.

"Stop it!" Vanity wiggled and giggled all over the bed.

"Hungry! I'll show you hungry." Dexter stopped tickling and pinned Vanity down. He spread her legs open and nibbled on her clit until she calmed down. Before long, Vanity hands were in his hair. Not to guide him, he did not need that. She connected with him. "Oooh," Vanity let out soft sounds. "Hmmm." Dexter did not waste time getting her climax. "Ahhh, Ahhh, Ahhh!" Vanity panted to catch her breath.

"Now, what were you saying?" Dexter said blowing a whisper onto her hot pussy.

"Hmmm?" Vanity was without words. She laid there motionless and suddenly no longer hungry.

Dexter came back up to the top of the bed, propped his head up on his hand and looked down at Vanity.

"Are you ready for the grand opening?"

Vanity was shocked at the question but she went with it, "Yes. Everything is in place." The change of subject gave Vanity a little relief. All of the relationship talk was making her nervous. Her stall in the car the night before was to gain a little more time to decide if this is what she wanted to do.

"Can I assist with anything?"

"Actually, you can. I am going to have a meeting with my local partners and I'd like you to manage this location."

"Why? Why aren't you going to do it?"

"Dexter, I have not decided to stay in London. This is not my home. My daughter and my businesses are back in the States."

"What do I have to do to convince you to stay?"

"Dexter, at this moment. Nothing. I appreciate all of this. I still love you and everything, b…"

"But what?" Dexter finished.

"Love hurts. I do not want to have that void in my heart again. I was just starting to recover."

"With Grant? Why did you agree to marry him if you did not want to be in love again?"

"That's just it. I do not love him the way I love you. Losing you was the worst feeling I have ever had in my life. Grant was someone I trusted to love and spend my time with so I could start to heal.

"Why are you hanging onto him?"

"He is safe or should I say, he was safe. I did not have to sacrifice my heart to be with him. We were just living one day at a time and love was just happening on its own. With you, my heart was on the line from day one."

"Vanity, your heart is still healing. It is still covered by the wall you built to protect it – from me."

"That about sums it up. So, now that we are all clear about my love life, are you going to manage the restaurant or not?" Vanity wanted to change the subject quickly.

"I'll do anything for you, Vanity. Of course, I will do it or hire someone to manage it. I can't talk you into staying and I obviously can't fuck you into staying either, so I guess I can help manage all of this money you're about to make." He managed a sincere laugh.

Dexter knew that Vanity needed more time. He genuinely appreciated her telling him the truth, especially about Grant. Vanity was still a healing soul.

thirteen

"Live from St. Christopher's, its Londontown's Burlesque!" The announcer said as the audience erupted in cheer for the opening act.

Vanity wore her new signature color for the grand opening, a white A-line dress by Versace. Dexter accompanied her in his teal blue Brioni Vanquish II. They were the couple to envy or at least that is what the crowd thought they were.

After the hotel seduction Dexter pulled, Vanity kept her distance. Dexter did not seem to mind as long as Vanity was in London. They started working together for the first time. Their work ethic was about the same. They had high expectations of their restaurant staff and because of his family name; Dexter had an image to uphold.

During the show, Vanity thought back on the last couple of weeks leading up to the opening and smiled at the outcome. Dexter tried to change several plans but Vanity had to convince him of her vision. His buy-in was not required but Vanity felt as if she needed him to feel like a partner in order for him to stay involved after she went back to the States. It was important for her to show him that he would be running things.

"Van, that's not a good strategy. Why haven't you thought about using recipes from Chef Fuchette?"

"Dexter, trust me. I have. The problem is his recipes are in fifty percent of our stores and I want to utilize Chef Rosario this time." Vanity rolled her eyes in frustration that Dexter wanted to make such a major change at the last minute.

"Who is Rosario? I haven't heard of him?"

"First of all, it is a *her* and you would not because you have not been running this business, I have. Rosario is an experienced chef and I am certain you will approve. I have scheduled a tasting for you. Rosario will be here in two days."

"Good, I have to see about this." Dexter continued to look through the rest of the grand opening plans.

"Anything else you want to know before we get down to the opening day?"

"I'll finish going over these plans and let you know. Hey, I have to get back to the estate. Can I take these?" Dexter held up the plan.

"Yes. I'll need any concerns brought back to me before the end of the week." Vanity stated.

"Great."

From that day, Dexter and Vanity operated in the vain as business partners. They spent the next week and a half meeting to fine-tune the plans.

Vanity was brought back to reality when the audience applauded for the first act of the night. She tried to mingle but the guests were very much into the show and Vanity thought that socializing would ruin the mood. Dexter seated next to her was equally as engaged.

"I take it you like the show." Vanity leaned over and whispered.

"I do actually. Great choice." Dexter said and immediately put his eyes back to the stage for the second act.

At intermission, the food was served and Vanity took that time to go check on the kitchen and staff. The demand for the grand opening was very high. Chef Rosario's menu was a big hit.

Several hours later, the guest finally started to leave and the staff clocked out to go home. Dexter and Vanity locked up the office and started to head home themselves. The London opening was a complete success.

"Vanity, what a night. I haven't felt this much excitement since we opened up St. Christopher's in Las Vegas," Dexter started. "You have really stepped it up a notch with the live shows." He said.

"Yea, some night." Vanity did not want to think about that night in Vegas. It was the night he was taken and nearly beaten to death. Dexter must have noticed the somber look on her face recalling that night.

"Vanity, come here." Dexter said before Vanity pressed the security code to lock up.

Vanity turned and came over to Dexter who was only a few feet away.

"You look so beautiful in this gown." He grabbed her hand, "I cannot apologize anymore for loving you until the true death of my life," Dexter looked into Vanity's eyes as he kneeled down on one knee.

The streetlights from outside were spotlighting the couple inside the restaurant. The only sounds they heard were the few cars on the street. The moment was simply all theirs.

Dexter pulled the ring from his pocket. Vanity looked down at him and the ring. The rarest gemstone in the world, the Alexandrite. The light from the street caused it to change color right before her eyes.

"Vanity Rodriquez, will you be my wife?" Dexter grabbed her hand and put the ring up to her finger. He looked in to her eyes with plead. He could not force it on her but he could not let her go without asking.

"Dexter, I love you. I have always loved you. I will always love you." Vanity stated while Dexter waited for his answer.

To Dexter it felt like an eternity before Vanity gave him an answer. He knew she did not want to live in London but he knew he could not ever go back to the States. Her choice would be his last chance.

Vanity could feel the tears burning in her eyes. The sacrifice to love this man was so great. It always was. The moment had arrived and she could only do what felt right. Vanity had to stay true to herself.

"Dexter…"

epilogue

"Stop running you two!" Cole yelled at the twins on her way to the dressing room. Cassidy and Collin ignored their mother and ran up the aisle of the church. Cole smiled at watching her children having a good time.

Vanity and Christina were putting on the final touches to their makeup when Cole entered. "Are you two ready?"

"Just about." Christina said.

"You two look beautiful," Cole said.

"Is my mother and grandmother here yet?" Vanity asked.

"Yes, they are in the sanctuary. We're all ready and waiting." Cole assured her.

"Okay, okay. I need a minute to talk to Chris." Vanity started to fan herself with the wedding program.

"Is everything OK, mom?" Christina asked.

"Yes, honey. I just want to make sure you're OK with this."

"Mom...we've been through this. Everything will be fine. Let's go." Christina said.

"Are you OK?" A man's voice came from the other side.

"We're fine. We are just about ready." Vanity said.

"What's taking so long?" He insisted and knocked again.

Within minutes, Vanity and her daughter Christina emerged. Cole smiled and tried to hold back tears as she stepped between her parents at the opening of the sanctuary. Everyone stood and the organ began to play.

❤❤❤

Love on Fire

SEVERAL YEARS LATER

Nicole

After much convincing Cole decided to let the twins spend the spring and summer breaks in London with the McKnight's. It was a much-needed break and it was only right to allow them to grow up knowing about their heritage. Little Prince Collin was the talk of the town. Cole agreed to give legal rights back to Dexter as long as she could raise them as her own.

Christina

After the wedding, Christina and her new husband moved into the home that her parents once shared in Vegas with the perfect view of the mountains set to the west. Vanity liked the idea of keeping it in the family especially with her first grandbaby on the way.

V. Marie

Clayton

He had taken up a new hobby. Fishing. It was quiet and he did not have to keep looking over his shoulder or checking surveillance cameras all day looking over someone else's shoulder. Life was good. After the last "job", he and Dexter planned never to see each other again.

Francine

Six feet below the surface of the earth, Francine sulked in her own pity. She clung onto sanity with the books and games she could play in the bunker. The only human she had any contact with wore a butler outfit and spoke with a British accent.

Dexter

Dexter's new identity allowed him to have some limelight in town. He ran St. Christopher's to stay busy and he always kept his hand in the family business. He spent summers with Prince Collin and Cassidy and took trips around the world to pass the time. Life became simple for Dexter, yet he missed the piece of his soul that left him – this time.

Love on Fire

Vanity

After leaving London, Vanity eventually sold her shares of St. Christopher's back to the McKnight's. It was a hard decision but it was the right thing to do. It felt as if a weight lifted from her. VanCole was her baby and her business. Going back was one of the best decisions she had ever made.

After three years of being back at the top of her marketing game, Vanity was comfortable with life and was ready for whatever came her way.

On the eve of her birthday, Vanity took a much-needed solo vacation to the Netherland Antilles. She checked into the most beautiful beach resort she had ever seen. The cool breeze whipped her flowing white dress and shuffled her hair as she walked. The straw hat she wore was no match for the breeze as it flew off her head scurrying down the walkway behind her.

"I'll get that for you ma'am." The man said coming up behind her.

Vanity turned around to greet and thank the nice man and nearly lost her balance.

"Hi." Her heart skipped a beat and the tickling butterfly in her stomach put a smile on her face.

He smiled back and placed the straw hat back on her head. He stared into her eyes longer than he should have. Vanity could not help but to reciprocate.

He did not ask...he did not wait...he leaned in and deeply kissed Vanity as they stood in the middle of the resort breezeway. A view of the ocean cascaded between them. The butterflies continued to flutter with excitement.

"Ask me again." She whispered.

"Vanity," he held her face in the palm of his hand, looking deeply into her eyes. "Will you be my wife?"

Without hesitation she answered, "Yes, my King. I will."

A sigh of relief escaped his mouth and he placed a soft kiss in the center of her forehead, then laid her head on his chest and embraced her securely.

Without a word spoken between them, they turned toward the ocean to appreciate its representation of endless possibilities and life's journey that brought them back together for a real chance at happiness.

The End

"Love recognizes no barriers. It jumps hurdles, leaps fences, penetrates walls to arrive at its destination full of hope."

– Maya Angelou

V. Marie

Acknowledgements

To the creator of life, love and happiness, I am thankful for all of which I have the pleasure of enjoying daily.

Before publishing my first book, I was afraid to let other people read my work. I would write books and read them myself – corky, huh? It was absolutely the scariest thing I have ever done – to publish my first book for the world.

This work was even tougher. I have fans now! They expect a great story and the pressure is on for it to be good, make sense and of course keep them on the edge of their seats. Having the faculty needed to express my imagination is a gift I will NEVER take for granted. To have control over my thoughts and putting them together for an exciting story is a gift. I appreciate my gift and thank everyone who supports it.

To my fans, friends and family in the US and abroad who supported my first book, I want to thank you for giving me the encouragement and motivation to continue writing.

About the Author

V. Marie was born and raised in Columbus, Ohio. V. Marie remembers writing her first book in grade school, titled, "All About Me". The book made with colored paper, affixed by Elmer's® glue, tape, staples and written in pencil, is in a box, still intact as a reminder of how early talents are born. Poems and love letters from high school fill other boxes to support her belief in love and the never-ending possibility of happiness. Who would have ever thought that thirty years later, she would be sharing that talent with the world.

V. Marie hopes you have become a fan *of life for life*. That is the ultimate message. She believes that life is meant to be lived and <u>you</u> will either live it vivaciously – or not and happiness is a state of mind and <u>you</u> will either be it – or not. <u>You</u> choose.

***

If you have enjoyed "Love on Fire", then you will love the freshman novel to this duo called "Love, Fire & Ice". The author would love to hear your review on the website at AuthorVMarie.com.

V. Marie

Book Club Discussion

1. If you read the first book, Love Fire & Ice, did the story line of this sequel keep you engaged?

2. How did characters change or evolve throughout the course of the story? What events trigger such changes?

3. What emotions (if any) did you feel during the book and at what points during the story?

4. If one (or more) of the characters made a choice that had moral implications, would you have made the same decision? Why? Why not?

5. Did you feel that the book fulfilled your expectations? Were you disappointed?

6. How did the book compare to other books in the same genre?

7. What do you think the main character learned by the end of the book?

8. In what ways do the events in the book reveal evidence of the author's view of life or the world?

9. Did certain parts of the book make you uncomfortable? If so, why did you feel that way? Did this lead to a new understanding or awareness of some aspect of your life you may not have thought about before?

10. Did the book end the way you expected?

Discussion Answers

www.ingramcontent.com/pod-product-compliance
Lightning Source LLC
Chambersburg PA
CBHW020441270626
47155CB00022B/793